Dream Big, Little Girl:

31 Stories to Inspire Your Young Lady to Achieve Great Heights in Life

All Original Stories By: Michael Gunning

Illustrations by: Michael Gunning,

Artie Fashell and Della Jantz

Copyright © August 2024

NY Publishing LTD

New York Charlotte Atlanta

First Edition

ISBN: 9798336836479

Library of Congress 2024914048

All rights reserved. No part of this publication may be reproduced, distributed, or transmitted in any form or by any means, including photocopying, recording, or other electronic or mechanical methods, without the prior written permission of the publisher, except in the case of brief quotations embodied in critical reviews and certain other noncommercial uses permitted by copyright law.

Welcome to "Dream Big Little Girl: 30 Stories to Inspire Your Young Lady to Achieve Great Heights in Life" This enchanting book is a collection of tales crafted especially for young girls, designed to ignite their imaginations and instill the belief that they can achieve anything their hearts desire. Each story introduces a unique heroine, brave and spirited, who embarks on exciting journeys filled with challenges and triumphs.

From Mia, the soccer star who helps her teammates to reach the stars, to Stella, the young artist who paints her dreams into reality, these stories are woven with rich imagery that allows readers to envision vibrant landscapes and colorful characters. Naomi, the nature-loving girl, discovers a hidden forest sanctuary, teaming up with animals to protect the environment. Each character reflects the many facets of girlhood—from playfulness to determination, creativity to compassion.

As you dive into the pages, you'll find stories laced with gentle wisdom and empowering messages. Whether it's overcoming fears, celebrating kindness, or exploring creativity, each narrative encourages girls to recognize their strengths. With each turn of the page, they will meet trailblazing women from history and whimsical, fictional and non-fictional characters who show them that it's not just enough to dream; they must also take action, believing wholeheartedly in themselves.

The stories have been thoughtfully crafted using accessible language and engaging plots, ensuring that young girls are not only entertained but inspired. Each story paints a picture, inviting little ones to visualize their adventures. Imagine Emma flying high above the clouds on a brightly colored kite, or Sofie the heroic brave mermaid saving the sailors of a doomed ship. These vivid illustrations will dance in their minds long after the final page has been read.

“Dream Big” is more than a collection of bedtime stories; it is a celebration of girlhood and the limitless ambitions that exist within every young girl. It seeks to create an environment where bravery and kindness flourish. In a world where they often see limitations, we want to remind girls that they can be scientists, artists, leaders, explorers, and so much more. They are capable of achieving greatness just by believing in themselves.

As the moon rises high, and sleepy eyes begin to flutter closed, let these tales of courage and kindness weave their magic. May the lessons learned from bold heroines echo in the dreams of young girls everywhere, guiding them as they weave their own stories and embark on their journeys. With a heart full of courage and imagination, every girl is destined to soar. Through the pages of this book, may they discover the extraordinary girl inside themselves, waiting to break free and shine bright.

So snuggle up, and let the stories begin. Dream big, little ones; the world is yours to explore!

Table of Contents

The Lost Lullaby

In a cozy bedroom filled with twinkling stars and soft moonlight, little Sophie tossed and turned. Her favorite toys watched from the shelf, worried about their friend.

"She can't sleep," whispered Teddy, a fluffy brown bear. "She misses her special lullaby."

"But Sophie's mommy forgot the words," said Dolly, smoothing her polka-dot dress. "What can we do?"

Suddenly, Rocket the toy spaceship had an idea. "Let's find the lost lullaby!" he exclaimed. "We'll search the whole house if we have to!"

The toys nodded in agreement. They carefully climbed down from the shelf and began their adventure.

First, they checked under Sophie's bed. Dust Bunny, who lived there, hadn't heard the lullaby.

"But I'll help you look!" he said, hopping along.

They tiptoed into the hallway, where Clock ticked softly on the wall.

"Time is precious," he chimed. "The lullaby might be in the attic, where old memories are stored."

Up the creaky stairs they went, with Teddy leading the way. In the attic, they found Box, who was full of Sophie's baby things.

"I remember that lullaby," Box creaked. "It was about stars and dreams and love. But I can't recall the words."

The toys didn't give up. They searched the whole house, from the kitchen to the living room, but couldn't find the lost lullaby.

Feeling sad, they returned to Sophie's room. But then, Dolly had an idea.

"Maybe we don't need to find the exact words," she said. "We could make a new lullaby, just for Sophie!"

Everyone agreed. Teddy hummed a gentle tune, Rocket added some "whoosh" sounds, and

Dust Bunny provided a soft rhythm. Dolly and Box sang about stars twinkling and sweet dreams, while Clock kept the beat.

As they sang their new lullaby, Sophie's eyes began to flutter closed. A smile spread across her face as she drifted off to sleep.

The toys climbed back onto the shelf, proud of what they had accomplished together.

"We may not have found the old lullaby," Teddy whispered, "but we created something even more special."

"A lullaby made with love," Dolly added softly.

And as the night grew deeper, the toys fell asleep too, dreaming of their adventure and the beautiful music they had made together.

From that night on, whenever Sophie had trouble sleeping, her toys would sing their special lullaby, filling the room with love and sweet dreams.

The Snoring Symphony

Once upon a time, a long time ago, little Emma couldn't sleep. She tossed and turned in her bed, trying to find the perfect cozy spot.

But something was keeping her awake. From all around the house came strange sounds.

Snooooore rumbled from her parents' room, like a far-off thunderstorm.

Whiffle-snort whistled from her brother Jack's room, reminding her of a tiny train chugging along.

Puff-puff-wheeze floated up from the living room, where Grandpa had fallen asleep in his favorite armchair.

Even Moe, the family dog, added his own *woof-snuffle* from his bed in the kitchen.

At first, Emma thought all this noise would keep her up all night. But then, something magical began to happen.

She closed her eyes and listened closely. The sounds started to change.

Dad's deep *snooooore* became the smooth, low notes of a cello, providing a steady beat.

Jack's *whiffle-snort* turned into the playful tune of a flute, dancing up and down in pitch.

Grandpa's *puff-puff-wheeze* transformed into the gentle rhythm of drums, keeping time for everyone else.

And Moe's *woof-snuffle* became the cheerful toot of a trumpet, adding little bursts of joy to the music.

Emma giggled softly. Her family wasn't just snoring – they were making music!

She imagined them all in fancy suits and dresses, standing on a big stage. Dad held a shiny cello, Jack had a silver flute, Grandpa sat behind a set of drums, and Moe (wearing a little bowtie) held a golden trumpet in his paws.

In her mind, Emma saw herself step onto the stage in a sparkling dress. She raised her arms like a conductor, and her family began to play.

The music swelled and swirled around her, filling the room with beautiful melodies. It was the most wonderful concert she had ever heard.

As Emma conducted, she felt her eyelids growing heavy. The music became softer and softer, like a gentle lullaby.

She imagined herself taking a bow as the audience clapped. Then she stepped off the stage and snuggled into a big, cozy bed right there in the concert hall.

The music of her family's snores continued to play softly, surrounding her like a warm blanket.

Emma yawned and smiled. "Goodnight, Snoring Symphony," she whispered, her eyes closing at last.

As she drifted off to sleep, the sounds of her family's snores blended together in perfect harmony. And if you listened very carefully, you might have heard a new sound join in – Emma's own tiny *snooooore*, like the softest string on a violin, completing the family orchestra.

From that night on, whenever Emma heard her family snoring, she didn't mind at all. Instead, she would smile and think of her own special symphony, playing just for her as she sailed off to dreamland.

And so, my little one, as you close your eyes tonight, listen closely. You might just hear your very own snoring symphony, ready to play you the sweetest lullaby of all.

Sweet dreams.

The Blanket Fort Adventure

Once upon a time, in a cozy little house at the end of Maple Street, there lived two siblings named Max and Lily. Max was eight years old and loved to build things, while six-year-old Lily had a huge imagination and could dream up the most amazing stories.

One rainy Saturday afternoon, Max and Lily were bored. "Let's build a blanket fort!" Max suggested excitedly.

Lily's eyes lit up. "Yes! And we can pretend it's a magical castle!"

They gathered all the blankets and pillows they could find, and with Mom and Dad's help, they created the most magnificent blanket fort in the living room.

It had tunnels and towers, secret passages and cozy nooks.

As night fell and it was time for bed, Max and Lily begged to sleep in their fort.

"Just for tonight," Mom said with a smile. "Sweet dreams, my little adventurers."

Max and Lily snuggled into their sleeping bags, whispering and giggling in the dark.

Suddenly, Lily gasped. "Max, look! The blankets... they're glowing!"

Sure enough, the walls of their fort were shimmering with a soft, magical light. Then, right before their eyes, the entrance to the fort transformed into a golden doorway.

"Should we go through?" Max asked nervously.

"Of course!" Brave Lily replied, her voice filled with excitement.

Hand in hand, the siblings stepped through the glowing doorway. In an instant, they found themselves standing on a beach with pink sand and purple waves.

The sky was filled with two suns – one blue and one green.

"Wow!" they exclaimed in unison. They spent what felt like hours building sandcastles and splashing in the warm purple water.

Just as they were getting tired, the golden doorway appeared again. They stepped through and were back in their blanket fort, cozy and warm.

"That was amazing," Max yawned. "I wonder where we'll go tomorrow night?"

The next night, their blanket fort took them to a world made entirely of candy. They slid down peppermint slides and bounced on marshmallow clouds.

The night after that, they found themselves in a world where animals could talk. They had tea with a family of rabbits and helped a squirrel find his lost acorn.

Each night was a new adventure, but no matter how exciting their journey, the magical doorway always brought them safely back to their cozy blanket fort.

One morning at breakfast, Mom asked, "You two have been sleeping so well in that fort. What's your secret?"

Max and Lily just smiled at each other.

"Let's just say we've been having magical dreams," Lily replied with a wink.

That night, as Max and Lily settled into their sleeping bags, they wondered what new world they might visit.

But as they drifted off to sleep, they realized something important: no matter how amazing their adventures were, the best part was always coming home to their family and their cozy blanket fort.

And so, Max and Lily's blanket fort adventures continued, filling their nights with wonder and their days with excited whispers of where they might go next.

But they always kept their magical secret, for they knew that sometimes, the most special magic is the kind you share just with your brother or sister.

Sweet dreams, little ones. Who knows what adventures await in your dreams tonight?

The Sleepy Spell Book

Once upon a time, in a cozy cottage at the edge of the Whispering Woods, there lived a young witch named Luna. Luna had sparkling eyes, a button nose, and a pointy hat that was just a bit too big for her head.

She loved nothing more than practicing her magic spells.

But Luna had a problem. Every time she tried to cast a spell, it would make things wake up instead of fall asleep! When she waved her wand at her stuffed bear, it would jump up and start dancing.

When she tried to quiet the chirping birds outside her window, they would burst into loud, cheerful songs.

"Oh dear," Luna would sigh, "how will I ever become a proper witch if I can't even cast a simple sleeping spell?"

One day, Luna's grandmother came to visit. Granny Moonbeam was the wisest witch in all the land, with silver hair that shimmered like starlight.

"What's troubling you, my little lunaberry?" Granny Moonbeam asked, noticing Luna's frown.

Luna explained her problem, and Granny Moonbeam's eyes twinkled with understanding. From her bag, she pulled out an old, dusty book bound in soft purple leather.

"This, my dear," she said, "is the Sleepy Spell Book. It contains all the secrets to casting the most wonderful sleep spells. But remember, with great power comes great responsibility. You must only use these spells to help others."

Luna promised to use the book wisely, and Granny Moonbeam left her to study. For days and nights, Luna pored over the Sleepy Spell Book, practicing the gentle wand movements and memorizing the soothing words.

Finally, Luna felt ready to try her new spells. She started small, with a restless butterfly that couldn't seem to settle on a flower.

"Flutterby, flutterby, time to rest," Luna whispered, waving her wand in a slow, swirling motion. "Find a petal for your cozy nest."

To her delight, the butterfly's wings slowed, and it gently landed on a soft daisy petal, quickly falling into a peaceful sleep.

Encouraged by her success, Luna ventured deeper into the Whispering Woods. She found a family of squirrels, chittering and unable to sleep because of a noisy owl.

"Shuffle and snuggle, little ones dear," Luna chanted softly. "Close your eyes, there's nothing to fear."

One by one, the little squirrels yawned, curled up in their tree hollow, and drifted off to sleep.

As Luna continued through the woods, she encountered more creatures in need of rest - a worried rabbit, a hiccuping frog, even the noisy owl himself.

With each spell, Luna's confidence grew, and she felt happiness bloom in her heart knowing she was helping others.

When Luna returned home, she found her own eyelids growing heavy. She changed into her favorite star-patterned pajamas and climbed into bed, hugging the Sleepy Spell Book to her chest.

"Thank you, Granny Moonbeam," Luna murmured sleepily. "I've learned that the best magic comes from kindness and helping others."

And with that, Luna closed her eyes and drifted off into a peaceful sleep, dreaming of all the creatures she had helped in the Whispering Woods.

From that day on, Luna became known as the kindest witch in all the land, always ready with a gentle spell to help any creature in need of a good night's sleep.

And as Luna sleeps in her cozy cottage, it's time for you to close your eyes too. May your dreams be filled with magic and kindness, just like Luna's.

Goodnight, sleep tight, and sweet dreams.

The Dreaming Pencil

Once upon a time, in a cozy little bedroom filled with colorful drawings, there lived a young girl named Jill. Jill loved to draw more than anything in the world.

Every night before bed, she would sketch a new picture with her favorite yellow pencil.

One evening, as Jill was getting ready for bed, she noticed something peculiar about her pencil.

It seemed to shimmer in the soft glow of her nightlight.

"How strange," she thought, but she was too sleepy to wonder much about it.

That night, as Jill drifted off to sleep, something magical happened. The yellow pencil began to twirl and dance across her sketchpad all on its own! It drew rolling hills, fluffy clouds, and a bright smiling sun.

As the pencil finished its drawing, a spectacular thing occurred – the picture began to come alive!

Jill found herself standing on top of one of the hills she had drawn. The grass tickled her toes, and a warm wind ruffled her hair.

She giggled with delight as she rolled down the hill, the soft grass cushioning her tumble.

At the bottom of the hill, she met a funny little creature with big ears and a fluffy tail.

"Hello!" it squeaked. "Welcome to Pencilvania! I'm Squiggle, and I'm here to show you around."

Jill and Squiggle spent the night exploring the wonderful world her pencil had created. They picked flowers that sang lullabies, slid down rainbows, and had a tea party with clouds that rained tiny candies.

As the dream-sun began to set, Jill knew it was time to go.

"Will I ever see you again, Squiggle?" she asked sadly.

Squiggle smiled and pointed to the yellow pencil that had appeared in Jill's hand.

"As long as you keep drawing, the Dreaming Pencil will bring your creations to life each night. You can visit anytime!"

Jill woke up the next morning, feeling happy and refreshed. She looked at her sketchpad and gasped – there was a new drawing of rolling hills and fluffy clouds, just like in her dream!

In the corner, she spotted a tiny signature that looked like a squiggle.

Every night after that, Jill would draw a new picture before bed. And every night, the Dreaming Pencil would bring her drawings to life, creating wonderful new worlds for her to explore in her dreams.

Sometimes she visited a castle in the clouds, where she had tea with a forgetful dragon.

Other nights, she swam in oceans made of blue jelly with friendly fish who told silly jokes. Each adventure was more amazing than the last.

Jill's parents noticed how excited she was to go to bed each night, and how her drawings seemed to get more and more imaginative.

They were happy to see their little girl so full of joy and creativity.

As Jill grew older, she never forgot about the Dreaming Pencil and the magical worlds it created. Even as an adult, she kept it close, using it to draw wonderful stories for her own children.

And who knows? Maybe one night, the Dreaming Pencil will choose to share its magic with them too.

So remember as you drift off to sleep tonight – your imagination is a powerful thing. Who knows what wonderful dreams it might create?

Close your eyes now, and let your own dreaming pencil draw you a magical world of adventures.

Sweet dreams!

The Pocket-Sized Explorer

In the pocket of your favorite jeans lives a tiny adventurer elf named Miranda. Not much bigger than your thumb, with wild red hair and bright green eyes, Miranda is always ready for an adventure.

During the day, Miranda sleeps snugly in your pocket, but at night, when the house is quiet and everyone is asleep, that's when Miranda's adventures begin.

Tonight, as the moon peeks through your bedroom window, Miranda climbs out of your pocket and slides down the side of your bed.

The floor stretches out like a vast plain, and Miranda sets off with a tiny backpack full of supplies.

First stop: the kitchen. Miranda scurries along the baseboards, watching out for any late-night pets that might be prowling. The refrigerator looms ahead like a shiny silver mountain.

Miranda uses a piece of string from the backpack to lasso the handle and climb up.

At the top, Miranda finds a feast! A droplet of milk becomes a refreshing pool to swim in. A crumb of cheese is as big as a house.

Miranda even discovers a giant raspberry and spends some time rolling it around like a ball.

After the snack, it's time to explore further. Miranda slides down the side of the fridge and heads for the living room.

The coffee table is like a huge, flat continent. Miranda finds a penny that had fallen between the couch cushions.

To someone as small as Miranda, it's as big as a shield!

Our tiny explorer practices rolling it around, pretending to be a knight in shining armor.

But wait! What's that sound?

Miranda freezes, holding the penny-shield up. It's just the house settling, creaking in the night.

Miranda giggles at being scared by such a silly thing.

Next, Miranda spots the houseplant in the corner. It's like a dense jungle, full of leaves as big as Miranda's whole body.

Carefully, our little adventurer climbs up the stem, swinging from leaf to leaf. At the top, Miranda can see the whole room spread out below.

What a view!

But the night is getting late, and Miranda is starting to feel sleepy. It's time to head back to the cozy jean pocket.

On the way, Miranda stops by the fireplace and picks up a bit of ash.

In Miranda's tiny hands, it's like a piece of chalk. Our explorer uses it to draw a little mark on the baseboard – a secret sign that means "Miranda was here."

Finally, Miranda climbs back up to your bed, tiny arms and legs tired from the night's adventure. Just as the first rays of sun start to peek through the window, Miranda snuggles back into your pocket, ready to dream about the next big adventure.

And in the morning, when you wake up, you might notice a tiny smudge on the baseboard or a penny in an odd place. You might wonder how they got there.

Miranda just smiles a secret smile from inside your pocket, already excited for the next nightly adventure in your home.

So tonight, as you drift off to sleep, remember that your home is full of wonder and adventure – all you need is a little imagination to see it.

Sweet dreams, little one. And who knows? Maybe you'll dream of pocket-sized adventures too.

Samantha the Dream Seeking Pegasus

Once upon a time, in a world not so different from our own, there was a gentle Pegasus named Samantha. Samantha wasn't like other flying horses.

While some flying horses rushed loudly and soared without purpose, Samantha preferred to whisper and wonder. You see, Samantha had a very special job – collecting and sharing bedtime stories from all around the world.

Every night, as the sun dipped below the horizon and the stars began to twinkle, Samantha would set off on a magical journey.

Floating over oceans and mountains, through bustling cities and quiet villages, Samantha listened carefully for the sound of bedtime stories being told.

One evening, Samantha drifted over a cozy igloo in the snowy Arctic. There, an Inuit grandmother was telling her grandchildren about Nanuk, the great polar bear who taught the people how to hunt and survive in the icy north.

Samantha listened closely, gathering every word like precious snowflakes.

Carrying the story of Nanuk, Samantha floated south to the warm savannas of Africa. In a small village, under a baobab tree, an elder was sharing the tale of Anansi the clever spider.

Samantha glided silently above the listeners, picking up Anansi's mischievous adventures.

Next, Samantha crossed the vast Pacific Ocean to a beautiful island in Japan. There, a father was telling his children about Kaguya-hime, the mysterious Moon Princess found inside a bamboo stalk.

Samantha gathered the story, feeling it shimmer like moonlight.

In the bustling streets of India, Samantha found a mother singing a lullaby about Krishna, the playful blue god who loved butter and played the flute.

The melody mixed with the story, creating a beautiful harmony in Samantha's collection.

As the night grew deeper, Samantha crossed the Atlantic to the lush Amazon rainforest. Deep in the jungle, a shaman was sharing the legend of how the colorful macaw got its rainbow feathers.

Samantha added this vibrant tale to the growing collection.

Finally, as the first light of dawn began to peek over the horizon, Samantha arrived at your window.

Gently pushing it open, Samantha entered your room, bringing with it the whispers of all the stories collected during the night's journey.

As you snuggle deeper into your warm bed, Samantha begins to softly whisper. You hear tales of brave polar bears and clever spiders, of mysterious moon princesses and mischievous gods, of colorful birds and ancient wisdom.

Each story is a little gift from a different part of the world, carried to you on the gentle breeze.

Samantha's whispers grow softer and softer as your eyes begin to close. The stories weave together in your dreams, creating a colorful tapestry of adventures from around the world.

As you drift off to sleep, you feel connected to all the other children who heard these same stories, in igloos and under baobab trees, in bamboo houses and jungle clearings.

And as the new day dawns, Samantha slips out of your window, ready to begin another night of collecting and sharing the world's bedtime stories.

For as long as there are stories to be told and children to hear them, Samantha, the dream seeking Pegasus, will continue its nightly journey, connecting us all through the magic of bedtime tales.

Sweet dreams, little one. Who knows what stories Samantha will bring tomorrow night?

The Midnight Garden

Once upon a time, in a cozy little house at the end of Willow Street, lived a curious girl named Abby. Abby loved to look out her bedroom window at night, watching the stars twinkle and the fireflies dance in her backyard.

One warm summer night, just as Abby was about to fall asleep, she heard the town clock strike twelve.

Bong, bong, bong! Abby sat up in bed, rubbing her eyes.

Was it morning already? But when she looked out her window, she gasped in wonder.

Her ordinary backyard had transformed into the most extraordinary garden she had ever seen!

The grass shimmered like emerald silk, and flowers of every color imaginable swayed gently in a soft, magical breeze.

Abby couldn't believe her eyes. She quietly tiptoed downstairs and out the back door, her bare feet sinking into the plush, cool grass.

As she stepped into the garden, she noticed the flowers were humming a gentle lullaby.

A rosebush nodded at her and whispered, "Welcome to the Midnight Garden, Abby."

Abby's eyes widened. "You can talk?"

The rose chuckled softly.

"Of course, dear. All flowers can talk in the Midnight Garden. But only special children like you can hear us."

Abby wandered through the garden, marveling at the wonders around her.

Butterflies with wings that glowed like rainbow crystals fluttered by.

A family of rabbits with fur as soft as clouds hopped past, wishing her a good evening.

In the center of the garden stood an enormous oak tree. Its branches reached up to the stars, and its leaves seemed to twinkle like tiny green lanterns.

"Hello, Abby," the oak tree's deep, kind voice rumbled. "We've been waiting for you."

"You have?" Abby asked, amazed.

"Indeed," the tree replied. "Every night at midnight, this garden comes to life, waiting for a child with a heart full of wonder and kindness to discover its magic."

Abby spent what felt like hours exploring the garden. She danced with the daisies, shared secrets with the snapdragons, and even had a tea party with a family of hedgehogs under a mushroom umbrella.

But as she yawned and rubbed her eyes, the oak tree gently said, "It's time for you to return to bed, little one. But don't worry, the Midnight Garden will be here whenever you need a little magic in your life."

Abby nodded sleepily and made her way back to the house. As she climbed into bed, she heard the town clock strike one.

Bong!

She looked out her window one last time, seeing her familiar backyard once again.

Was it all a dream? But then she noticed a single, shimmering petal on her windowsill and smiled.

The Midnight Garden was real, and it would be there, waiting for her, whenever she needed a little bit of magic.

As Abby drifted off to sleep, she could almost hear the flowers singing their lullaby, carried on the gentle night breeze.

And she knew that from that night on, her dreams would be filled with the wonders of the Midnight Garden.

Sweet dreams, little one. May your night be as magical as Abby's Midnight Garden.

The Bedtime Blob

Once upon a time, in a cozy little bedroom not so different from yours, there lived a child named Dorothy.

Dorothy loved bedtime stories and snuggly pajamas, but sometimes, falling asleep could be a bit tricky.

One night, as Dorothy was tossing and turning, unable to drift off to dreamland, something magical happened.

A soft, shimmering light appeared at the foot of the bed, and from it emerged a curious creature: the Bedtime Blob!

The Blob was unlike anything Dorothy had ever seen. It was round and squishy, like a big marshmallow, and it glowed with a gentle, soothing light.

Its color shifted softly between calming shades of white and purple.

"Hello, Dorothy," the Blob said in a voice as soft as a whisper. "I'm here to help you fall asleep."

Dorothy sat up, eyes wide with wonder. "How can you help me sleep?"

The Blob wiggled happily. "I can shape myself into anything you need to feel comfortable and relaxed. What would help you sleep tonight?"

Dorothy thought for a moment. "Sometimes, I like to hug my teddy bear when I can't sleep."

No sooner had Dorothy said this than the Blob began to change. It stretched and molded itself until, right before Dorothy's eyes, it had become a big, cuddly teddy bear!

"How's this?" the Blob-bear asked.

Dorothy giggled and hugged the soft, warm bear. It felt just right, and Dorothy could feel sleepiness starting to creep in.

But Dorothy wasn't quite ready for sleep yet. "That's nice, but sometimes I also like to listen to rain sounds."

The Blob-bear smiled and began to change again. This time, it flattened and spread out, becoming a fluffy cloud right above Dorothy's bed. Soft, pattering sounds filled the room, just like gentle rain on a roof.

Dorothy yawned, feeling even sleepier now. The rain sounds were so soothing.

"Is there anything else you need?" the Blob-cloud asked.

Dorothy thought hard. "Well, sometimes when I'm almost asleep, I like to look at the stars."

The Blob-cloud twinkled with delight. It began to break apart into tiny, glowing dots that floated up to the ceiling.

Soon, Dorothy's entire room was filled with softly glowing "stars," twinkling and dancing in soothing patterns.

Dorothy lay back, watching the stars with heavy eyelids. It was so beautiful and peaceful.

The Blob's voice came again, soft and distant like a lullaby:

"Close your eyes, Dorothy. Let yourself drift off to sleep. I'll be here, watching over you all night long."

Dorothy's eyes fluttered closed, a smile on their face. The Bedtime Blob's starlight glow grew softer and softer, and the gentle rain sounds faded to a quiet hush.

Just before drifting off completely, Dorothy whispered, "Thank you, Bedtime Blob."

And as Dorothy fell into a deep, restful sleep, the stars above twinkled their reply: "Sweet dreams, Dorothy. Sweet dreams."

From that night on, whenever Dorothy had trouble sleeping, the Bedtime Blob would appear. Sometimes it was a cozy blanket, other times a gently rocking cradle.

No matter what shape it took, it always brought comfort and sweet dreams.

And so, my little one, as you lie here now, imagine your own Bedtime Blob. What shape would it take to help you sleep?

Maybe it's a fluffy cloud, or a soft, cuddly animal. Whatever it is, let it fill your mind with peace and calm.

Close your eyes and take a deep breath. Feel yourself getting heavier and sleepier. The Bedtime Blob is here, watching over you, keeping you safe and comfortable all through the night.

Sweet dreams, my love. Sweet dreams.

The Pajama Parade

Once upon a time, in a cozy little bedroom not so different from yours, there lived a young girl named Annie. Annie loved bedtime, not just because she got to snuggle up with her favorite stuffed bear, Mr. Fluffles, but because of a magical secret she discovered one night.

You see, every evening after Annie fell asleep, something extraordinary happened.

Her pajamas, the ones she had worn the night before and tossed into the laundry basket that morning, would come to life!

It started one night when Annie woke up to get a glass of water. As she tiptoed back to her room, she heard a soft shuffling sound.

Peeking through the crack in her door, she saw the most amazing sight.

Her pajamas, the ones with little yellow ducks all over them, were marching around the room!

The pajama top was leading the parade, its sleeves waving like a conductor's arms. The pajama bottoms followed, hopping along in a silly dance.

Annie rubbed her eyes, sure she must be dreaming. But no, the pajama parade was real!

As she watched, fascinated, she realized the pajamas weren't just marching randomly. They were acting out scenes from yesterday!

The pajama top flew around the room like the kite Annie had flown in the park yesterday afternoon. The bottoms crouched down and then sprang up, just like when Annie had played leapfrog with her friends.

Every night after that, Annie would pretend to fall asleep, then secretly watch the pajama parade.

Each pair of pajamas she wore would come alive and tell the story of the day before.

Her rocket ship pajamas zoomed around the room, remembering the trip to the science museum.

Her flower-print nightgown twirled and swayed, reliving the dance class Annie had taken.

One night, Annie wore her favorite unicorn pajamas. She had a wonderful day at school, where she learned to write her name and drew a picture of her family.

The next night, the unicorn pajamas put on quite a show!

The pajama top used its horn to write "ANNIE" in the air with sparkly magic. Then, the pajama bottoms stood on their leg ends and used the sleeves of the top to draw a family portrait, just like Annie had done in class.

Annie giggled quietly, amazed at how the pajamas remembered every detail of her day.

But the pajama parade wasn't just about fun and games. Sometimes, it helped Annie too.

One day, Annie had a small argument with her best friend, Emma.

The next day, Annie was so sad because of the fight but didn’t know what to do. Her best friend Emma didn’t even sit at her table during lunch time.

But that night, her striped pajamas acted out the scene. The top and bottoms faced away from each other, just like Annie and Emma had done.

But then, the pajamas turned around and gave each other a big hug. Annie smiled, realizing that's exactly what she should do the next day.

And she did!

Emma and Annie made up, and their friendship was stronger than ever.

As time went on, Annie began to look forward to bedtime more and more. She loved reliving the best parts of her days through the pajama parade.

It made her appreciate all the little moments that made each day special.

And you know what? The pajamas seemed to enjoy it too! Sometimes, Annie thought she could hear tiny giggles coming from her laundry basket as she drifted off to sleep.

So tonight, as you put on your pajamas and climb into bed, remember Annie's magical secret. Who knows? Maybe your pajamas are getting ready for their own parade, eager to celebrate all the wonderful things you did yesterday.

Sweet dreams, and may your own pajama parade be full of joy and wonder!

The Star Collector

In a cozy house on top of a hill lived a little girl named Luna. Every night, Luna would climb up to her roof with her telescope and gaze at the stars.

She knew all their names and could point out every constellation in the sky.

One warm summer night, as Luna peered through her telescope, she saw something unusual. A tiny star was zooming across the sky, leaving a trail of sparkles behind it.

"A shooting star!" Luna gasped. But instead of disappearing, the star swooped down and hovered right in front of her.

"Hello," said the star in a twinkling voice. "I'm Ziggy, and I'm lost. Can you help me find a home?"

Luna was amazed. She'd never talked to a star before!

"Of course," she said. "But where did you come from?"

Ziggy sighed, his light dimming a little.

"I used to be part of the Big Dipper, but I fell out. Now I don't know where I belong." he said sadly.

Luna thought for a moment.

"I have an idea," she said. "Why don't we find you a new constellation to join?"

Ziggy brightened up.

"Really? You'd do that for me?"

Luna nodded, smiling. "That's what friends are for!"

From that night on, Luna became known as the Star Collector. Word spread among the shooting stars, and they started visiting her every night.

There was Twinkle, who was too shy to shine brightly in the Big Dipper. Luna introduced her to the gentle stars of the Little Dipper, where Twinkle found she could sparkle comfortably.

Then came Flash, an energetic star who was too fast for the slow-moving Ursa Major.

Luna helped him find a home in the swift-footed constellation of Leo, where he could zoom around to his heart's content.

Glimmer was a romantic star who felt out of place in the warrior-like Orion. Luna found her a perfect spot in Cassiopeia, where she could shine with other stars who loved to tell stories of love and beauty.

Each night brought new stars with new stories, and Luna listened to them all.

She learned that sometimes, stars didn't fit where they were born, and that was okay. There was always a place where they could belong and shine their brightest.

One night, a particularly sad star named Flicker floated down to Luna.

"What's wrong, Flicker?" Luna asked.

"I've visited every constellation," Flicker said softly. "But I don't fit in anywhere. I'm not bright enough, or fast enough, or anything enough."

Luna thought hard. She looked at all the constellations she knew, but couldn't think of the right place for Flicker. Then, she had an idea.

"Flicker," she said, "what if we made a new constellation, just for stars like you?"

Flicker's light pulsed with excitement. "Can we do that?"

"Of course!" Luna said. "We'll call it... Luna's Heart. It'll be a home for all the stars who haven't found their place yet."

Over the next few weeks, Luna and Flicker worked together. They invited other lost stars to join them, arranging them in the shape of a big, shining heart in the sky.

Soon, Luna's Heart became the brightest constellation in the sky. It was full of stars of all kinds – big and small, bright and dim, quick and slow.

But together, they created something beautiful.

From then on, whenever Luna looked up at the night sky, she saw not just patterns of stars, but a tapestry of friendship. And she knew that somewhere up there, in Luna's Heart, Ziggy, Twinkle, Flash, Glimmer, Flicker, and all their new star friends were twinkling back at her, happy in their new home.

As for Luna, she kept watching the skies every night. After all, you never know when another lost star might need a friend to help them find their way home.

Lumi the Lonely Lighthouse

Once upon a time, on a rocky cliff by the sea, stood Lumi, the lonely lighthouse. With its bright white walls and tall tower, Lumi shone like a beacon against the vibrant blue sky. But despite its beauty, Lumi often felt sad and lonely.

While the sun sparkled on the ocean waves, Lumi longed for the laughter and joy of the boats passing by and the cheerful townsfolk who lived beyond the cliffs.

Every night, as Lumi beamed its guiding light across the water, it wished for a friend.

"If only someone would visit me," Lumi sighed, its light dimming slightly as the sun dipped below the horizon.

The boats sailed past, their sailors too busy to notice the lonely lighthouse standing watch.

One sunny afternoon, a young girl named Melissa wandered along the rocky shore.

With her golden hair bouncing in the warm breeze and her bright blue dress fluttering like a flag, she loved exploring the coastline.

As she meandered closer to the cliff, she spotted Lumi standing tall and shimmering in the sunlight.

“Hello there!” Melissa called out, her voice filled with cheer. “You’re such a beautiful lighthouse!”

Lumi, surprised by the girl’s kindness, responded, “Thank you! But I’m so lonely here. I’ve never had a friend to talk to or play with. No one ever stops by.”

Melissa felt a pang of sadness for Lumi.

“Oh, I’m sorry! That must be lonely indeed. I promise to come and visit you often! I’ll bring you stories and laughter!”

Lumi’s light flickered with hope for the first time. “Really? You would do that for me?”

“Of course! And I have an idea,” Melissa replied excitedly. “Let’s make beautiful music together!”

Melissa climbed the winding path to the top of Lumi’s tower and sat down beside the light. “I love to hum and sing,” she said. “How about we hum and sing some wonderful hymns? We can pick one to be our special song! It will travel across the water and attract everyone nearby!”

Lumi felt a spark of joy. “I’ve never sung before! I’d love to try.”

With that, Melissa started to hum a sweet melody. Her voice danced through the air, and Lumi listened closely, trying to replicate the soothing hum. Soon they were in harmony, the sound woven together like a gentle ocean breeze.

As they sang, Melissa noticed something magical happening. The boats on the water began to slow down, their captains turning to listen.

Fishermen paused their work, and the townspeople, curious about the lovely music, began to gather at the shore.

Day after day, Melissa returned to Lumi, humming and singing beautiful hymns until the lighthouse glowed with happiness.

The boats came closer, and sailors smiled and waved. Townspeople cheered as they listened to the enchanting music floating through the air.

One evening, as the sun painted the sky with shades of pink and gold, a flurry of boats anchored near the shore, their riders clapping and calling out, “Thank you, Lumi! Your light and music guide us home!”

Lumi beamed with pride, its light shining brighter than ever.

"I've never felt so happy!" Lumi exclaimed. "All thanks to you, Melissa!"

The friendship between Lumi and Melissa blossomed, almost as bright as the lighthouse's light itself. Together, they filled the air with joy and laughter, teaching everyone that kindness and love could change the world around them.

And so, Lumi was no longer the lonely lighthouse. With Melissa by its side, it became a cherished symbol of friendship, guiding boats home and shining brightly in the hearts of everyone who passed by.

From that day forward, Lumi hummed its wonderful hymns, filled with the warmth of love,

making the seaside a happier place for all.

The lighthouse realized it would never be lonely again, thanks to the kindness of a girl named Melissa.

The Yawning Contest

Once upon a time, in a cozy forest where the trees whispered lullabies and the streams gurgled softly, there lived a group of friendly animals.

One lazy afternoon, as the sun began to dip behind the trees, casting long, sleepy shadows, the animals gathered in a clearing.

Ollie the Owl, who was usually asleep at this time, blinked his big eyes and said, "You know, I think I have the most contagious yawn in the whole forest."

Rabbit Rosie twitched her nose and replied, "Oh no, Ollie. My yawn is so contagious, it can make flowers close their petals!"

Bear Barney, who had just woken up from a nap, rumbled, "You're both wrong. My yawn is so big and contagious, it can make the trees sway!"

The animals began to argue, each claiming their yawn was the most contagious.

Finally, wise old Tortoise Tim slowly raised his wrinkled head and suggested, "Why don't we have a contest to see whose yawn truly is the most contagious?"

All the animals agreed this was a splendid idea. They decided that whoever could make the most animals yawn with a single yawn would be crowned the Yawn Champion of the Forest.

As the moon rose, casting a soft, silvery light over the clearing, the contest began.

First up was Ollie the Owl. He puffed up his feathers, opened his beak wide, and let out a soft "Hooo-ahhh-hooo." Two squirrels and a hedgehog immediately yawned in response.

Next came Rabbit Rosie. She wiggled her pink nose, stretched her long ears, and yawned a tiny "Eee-awww-eee." Three butterflies, a mouse, and a cricket all yawned after her.

Bear Barney lumbered to the center of the clearing. He stood up on his hind legs, stretched his big furry arms, and let out an enormous "GRRRR-AHHH-WRRR."

The yawn was so big that five birds, two foxes, and a family of deer all yawned in unison.

One by one, each animal took their turn. Sleepy Sloth Simon's slow-motion yawn made everyone feel like they were moving through honey.

Giraffe Gina's long-necked yawn seemed to stretch on forever.

Even tiny Ant Annie's microscopic yawn managed to make a few other insects yawn!

As the night wore on, more and more animals found themselves yawning, their eyelids growing heavy. The moonflowers began to open, filling the air with their sweet, dreamy scent.

Finally, it was Tortoise Tim's turn. He very slowly opened his mouth and began to yawn. "Ahh..." he started, his yawn building like a gentle wave. "Ahh..." it continued, growing softer and slower. "Ahhh..."

But before Tim could finish his yawn, a remarkable thing happened. The entire forest had fallen asleep! Every animal, from the tallest giraffe to the tiniest ant, was curled up and snoozing peacefully.

Tortoise Tim looked around with amusement.

"Well," he said to himself with a small smile, "I suppose we'll never know whose yawn was the most contagious after all."

And with that, Tim tucked his head into his shell and drifted off to sleep himself, joining the rest of the forest in peaceful slumber.

From that day on, whenever an animal in the forest had trouble falling asleep, they would remember the great Yawning Contest. They would think of Ollie's soft "Hooo-ahhh-hooo," Rosie's tiny "Eee-awww-eee," Barney's big "GRRRR-AHHH-WRRR," and all the other wonderful yawns.

And before they knew it, they'd be yawning too, drifting off into sweet dreams.

And so, my little one, as you lie here listening to this story, perhaps you feel a yawn coming on too. Your eyes might be getting a bit heavy, just like the animals in the forest.

And that's okay, because it's time for you to join the Yawning Contest too, and drift off into your own wonderful dreams.

Goodnight, sleep tight, and sweet dreams.

The Dream Delivery Service

In a cozy forest, not far from where you sleep, there's a special group of animals who only come out at night. They call themselves the Dream Delivery Service, and they have a very important job: to bring sweet dreams to all the sleeping children in the world.

The leader of this magical team is Oliver the Owl. With his big, round eyes and soft, silent wings, he can see in the dark and fly without making a sound.

Oliver organizes the team and makes sure every child gets the perfect dream.

Next is Bella the Bat. Her super-sensitive ears can hear the whispers of wishes that children make before they fall asleep. Bella tells the team what each child hopes to dream about.

Rusty the Red Panda is in charge of colors. With his bright red fur and clever paws, he paints the dreams with all the colors of the rainbow, making them vivid and beautiful.

Luna the Luna Moth sprinkles dream dust over the sleeping children. Her delicate, moon-shaped wings glow softly in the dark, helping to guide the team.

Finally, there's Whiskers the Mouse. Small and quick, Whiskers can squeeze through the tiniest gaps to deliver dreams to children in hard-to-reach places.

Every night, as the sun sets and the moon rises, the Dream Delivery Service gathers in a clearing in the heart of the forest.

Oliver hoots softly, calling the meeting to order.

"Alright, team," he says, his feathers ruffling in the gentle night breeze. "What dreams do we have to deliver tonight?"

Bella's ears twitch as she listens to the night air.

"Little Emma wishes for a dream about flying," she chirps. "And Tommy hopes to dream of being a brave knight."

Oliver nods wisely.

"Excellent. Rusty, can you prepare the colors for those dreams?"

Rusty salutes with his bushy tail.

"Of course! I'll use sky blue and cloud white for Emma's flying dream, and silver and gold for Tommy's knight adventure." Rusty said.

Luna flutters her glowing wings.

"I've got fresh dream dust ready to go," she says in her soft, whispery voice.

"Perfect," Oliver hoots. "And Whiskers, are you ready to make the deliveries?"

Whiskers stands up on his hind legs, whiskers twitching with excitement.

"Ready and willing, sir!"

With everything prepared, the team sets off into the night. Oliver leads the way, his silent wings cutting through the darkness.

Bella listens carefully, making sure they're heading in the right direction. Rusty carries his paints, leaving a trail of colorful paw prints in the sky.

As they reach each house, Luna sprinkles her dream dust over the sleeping children, while Whiskers scurries inside to place the dreams gently in their minds.

All through the night, the Dream Delivery Service works tirelessly. They visit houses in the countryside, apartments in busy cities, and cozy cabins in the mountains.

No child is ever forgotten.

As the first light of dawn begins to peek over the horizon, the team returns to their forest home, tired but happy. They snuggle up in their warm, comfy beds, knowing they've brought joy and wonder to children all over the world.

And so, as you close your eyes and drift off to sleep, listen carefully. You might hear the soft beat of Oliver's wings, or catch a glimpse of Luna's glowing form outside your window.

For the Dream Delivery Service is always out there, working hard to bring you the sweetest dreams they can find.

Remember, every dream is a special gift, crafted with love and care by this remarkable team of nighttime animals. So sleep tight, and get ready for tonight's magical delivery. Who knows what wonderful adventures await you in your dreams?

The Lullaby Echo

Once upon a time, in a far-off land where the mountains touched the sky, there was a deep and winding canyon. This canyon was very old and very lonely.

While the forests around it bustled with life and the nearby river sang merry songs, the canyon sat in silence, its tall walls echoing only the occasional gust of wind.

"Oh, how I wish I had a voice of my own," the canyon would think to itself. "Then maybe I wouldn't be so lonely."

Days turned into weeks, and weeks into months, but still, the canyon remained quiet and alone.

The birds didn't nest in its rocky walls, and the animals didn't seek shelter in its caves. It seemed that everyone preferred the lively forest or the musical river.

One day, as the sun was setting and painting the sky in beautiful shades of orange and pink, a group of travelers made their way along the canyon's rim.

They were tired from their long journey and decided to make camp for the night.

As the stars began to twinkle in the darkening sky, one of the travelers, a young girl with bright eyes and a kind smile, began to sing a lullaby.

Her voice was soft and sweet, floating gently on the evening wind.

The canyon, curious about this new sound, listened intently. And then, something magical happened. As the last notes of the girl's song faded away, the canyon found itself repeating the melody.

The sound bounced off its walls, growing softer and softer until it disappeared into the night.

The travelers were amazed. "Did you hear that?" they asked each other. "The canyon sang us a lullaby!"

The young girl, delighted, sang another song.

And once again, the canyon echoed it back, its rocky walls softening the notes into a gentle, soothing lullaby.

From that night on, the canyon was no longer silent. It had discovered its voice – an echo that could turn any song into a beautiful lullaby. Word spread quickly about the magical singing canyon, and soon, more travelers began to visit.

They would come from far and wide, tired from their journeys, seeking a peaceful place to rest.

And every night, the canyon would echo their songs back to them as lullabies, helping them drift off into peaceful slumber.

The birds, enchanted by the gentle echoes, began to build their nests in the canyon's nooks and crannies. Small animals found the sound soothing and made their homes in its caves.

Even the trees from the nearby forest started to grow along the canyon's rim, their leaves rustling in harmony with the echoed lullabies.

As time passed, the once-lonely canyon became a place of joy and rest. Travelers would speak fondly of the nights they spent there, lulled to sleep by the canyon's magical echoes.

Children would beg their parents to take the route through the singing canyon, excited to hear their own voices transformed into lullabies.

And the canyon, no longer lonely, was happy. It had found its purpose – to provide comfort and peaceful rest to all who visited.

Every night, as the sun set and the stars came out, the canyon would wait eagerly for new songs to echo, ready to sing the world to sleep.

So if you ever find yourself traveling through a deep and winding canyon, and you hear your own song echoing back to you as a gentle lullaby, you'll know you've found the magical Lullaby Echo.

And as you drift off to sleep, know that the canyon is watching over you, happy to have turned your song into a peaceful night time melody.

Now, close your eyes and imagine the soft echoes of the canyon singing you to sleep. Sweet dreams, little one.

The Moonlight Orchestra

In the heart of Whispering Woods, where the trees stood tall and the stars twinkled bright, there lived a group of nocturnal animals who loved nothing more than the sound of music.

But during the day, when all the other forest creatures were awake, they had to stay quiet and hide in their homes.

One night, as the moon rose high in the sky, casting a soft silver glow over the forest, a clever owl named Owen had an idea.

He flew from tree to tree, tapping gently on the homes of his nighttime friends.

"Psst, Melody," he whispered to a raccoon. "Bring your pebble shakers!"

"Riley," he called softly to a rabbit. "Don't forget your carrot flute!"

One by one, Owen gathered his friends in a moonlit clearing. There was Jasper the jazz-loving bat,

Harmony the hummingbird who hummed the sweetest tunes, and Tempo the tap-dancing fox.

"Friends," Owen hooted quietly, "I have a wonderful idea. Why don't we form an orchestra and play music for all the sleeping creatures of the forest?"

The animals looked at each other with excitement twinkling in their eyes. They had always wanted to share their music but never knew how.

"But Owen," Melody the raccoon asked, "won't we wake everyone up?"

Owen's eyes twinkled. "Not if we play softly, like a lullaby. Our music will weave into their dreams and give them the sweetest sleep they've ever had!"

And so, the Moonlight Orchestra was born. Every night, as the moon climbed high into the sky, the nocturnal animals would gather in the clearing.

Owen would conduct with a slender twig, his wide eyes watching carefully as each animal played their part.

Melody shook her pebble shakers with a gentle rhythm, while Riley blew soft notes on his carrot flute.

Jasper's wings fluttered in a jazzy beat, and Harmony's hum blended everything together in perfect harmony.

Tempo's paws tapped out a quiet beat on a fallen log.

As they played, something magical began to happen. The flowers in the clearing seemed to sway to the music, their petals opening a little wider to listen. The leaves on the trees rustled softly, as if they were whispering the melody to each other.

In their nests and dens, the sleeping animals began to smile in their sleep. Squirrels curled their tails a little tighter, feeling cozy and warm.

Baby birds snuggled closer to their mothers, dreaming of flying through cotton candy clouds.

Even grumpy old Mr. Badger, who usually complained about every little noise, found himself having the most wonderful dreams of dancing under the moonlight.

Night after night, the Moonlight Orchestra played their soothing songs. They learned new melodies from the wind whistling through the trees and composed tunes inspired by the twinkling stars.

As the seasons changed, so did their music. In summer, they played light, breezy songs that mimicked the sound of gentle streams.

In autumn, their melodies were rich and golden like the falling leaves. Winter brought soft, crystalline tunes that sounded like snowflakes falling, and in spring, their songs were as fresh and lively as new buds blooming.

One night, as they finished a particularly beautiful song, they heard a soft sound. At first, they thought it was just the wind, but then they realized – it was applause!

They looked around in surprise to see all the daytime animals standing at the edge of the clearing, smiling and clapping their paws softly.

"We woke up to the most beautiful music we've ever heard," said Mrs. Squirrel, her eyes shining. "We just had to see where it was coming from!"

From that night on, the Moonlight Orchestra played for both the sleeping and the awake, filling Whispering Woods with joy and music. And every animal, whether they were awake or asleep, had a smile on their face and a song in their heart.

So as you drift off to sleep tonight, listen closely. You might just hear the soft, sweet melodies of your very own Moonlight Orchestra, playing a lullaby just for you.

Sweet dreams, and may your night be filled with beautiful music.

The Bubble Bus

Lucy loved bubbles. She loved how they sparkled in the sunlight, how they floated gently on the wind, and how they made everything look magical when they popped.

But most of all, Lucy loved the Bubble Bus.

Every night, just as Lucy was getting ready for bed, she would hear a faint "pop-pop-pop" outside her window. She knew that sound.

It was Mr. Suds, the Bubble Bus driver, arriving on her street.

Lucy would rush to her window and wave.

Mr. Suds, with his curly white hair that looked like soap suds and his bright blue uniform covered in bubble patterns, would wave back with a smile.

"All aboard the Bubble Bus!" he would call softly, not wanting to wake the neighbors.

Lucy would close her eyes, and when she opened them, she found herself standing next to Mr. Suds in front of the most amazing bus she had ever seen.

It wasn't made of metal like regular buses. Oh no! The Bubble Bus was one enormous, shimmering soap bubble.

"Where shall we go tonight, Lucy?" Mr. Suds asked, his eyes twinkling.

"Can we visit the cloud castle?" Lucy replied excitedly.

"The cloud castle it is!" Mr. Suds declared, opening the bubble door with a wave of his bubble wand.

Lucy stepped inside, joining her friends Max, Zoe, and Oliver, who were already seated.

The seats were made of smaller bubbles that felt soft and bouncy.

With a gentle "pop," the Bubble Bus lifted off the ground and floated up into the night sky.

As they rose higher and higher, Lucy watched in wonder as the twinkling lights of the city grew smaller below them.

Suddenly, they were surrounded by fluffy white clouds. Mr. Suds steered the bus through a cloud that looked exactly like a castle gate. On the other side was a magical world made entirely of clouds.

Cloud people waved as the Bubble Bus passed by.

Lucy and her friends waved back, giggling at the cloud people's puffy hair and billowing clothes.

They saw cloud dogs chasing cloud cats, and cloud birds soaring through the sky. There were cloud flowers that changed colors as the wind blew through them, and even a cloud playground where cloud children were sliding down rainbows.

As they reached the center of the cloud world, they saw the magnificent cloud castle.

It was enormous, with towers that spiraled up so high they disappeared into the mist above.

Mr. Suds parked the Bubble Bus, and they all climbed out. The cloud ground felt squishy beneath Lucy's feet, like walking on a giant marshmallow.

They explored the castle, sliding down banisters made of sunbeams and bouncing on beds made of the softest clouds Lucy had ever felt.

In the castle kitchen, cloud chefs were whipping up dishes made of rainbows and moonbeams.

After what seemed like hours of fun, Mr. Suds called out, "Time to head home, children! We don't want to be late for bedtime."

As they climbed back into the Bubble Bus, the cloud people gathered to wave goodbye. The cloud king even gave them each a small cloud pillow as a souvenir.

The journey home was peaceful. As the Bubble Bus floated gently through the night sky, Lucy felt her eyes growing heavy.

She hugged her cloud pillow close, remembering all the wonderful things she had seen.

Just as she was about to drift off to sleep, Lucy felt a gentle "pop."

She opened her eyes to find herself back in her own bed, tucked in snugly with her cloud pillow still in her arms.

From her window, she could hear the faint "pop-pop-pop" of the Bubble Bus departing.

Lucy smiled, already excited for tomorrow night's adventure. As she snuggled deeper into her covers, she wondered where Mr. Suds and the Bubble Bus would take her next.

With happy thoughts of bubble journeys dancing in her head, Lucy closed her eyes and drifted off into a peaceful sleep, ready to dream of more magical adventures.

The Friendly Shadow

Once upon a time, in a cozy little house at the end of Maple Street, there lived a young girl named Maggie. Maggie was bright and curious, but she had one big fear: the dark.

Every night, when the lights went out, she would huddle under her blankets, imagining all sorts of scary things lurking in the shadows.

One particularly dark night, as Maggie lay trembling in her bed, she noticed something strange. Her shadow on the wall seemed to be... moving!

But that couldn't be right, could it? Shadows don't move on their own.

"Hello?" Maggie whispered, her voice shaky.

To her amazement, the shadow waved back!

Maggie rubbed her eyes in disbelief. "Can you... can you talk?" she asked.

The shadow nodded and then, in a voice as soft as a whisper, said,

"Hi Maggie. I'm Shade, your shadow. I've always been with you, but tonight I thought you might need a friend."

Maggie's fear began to melt away, replaced by curiosity.

"But how can you talk? And move?"

Shade chuckled, a sound like rustling leaves.

"Magic, of course! And a little bit of moonlight. I'm here to show you that the dark isn't scary at all. In fact, it can be quite fun!"

Maggie sat up in bed, intrigued. "Fun? How?"

"Well," said Shade, stretching tall on the wall, "why don't we go on an adventure and find out?"

Hesitantly,Maggie climbed out of bed. As her feet touched the floor, she felt a warm, comforting presence beside her. It was Shade, no longer on the wall but standing right next to her like a friend holding her hand.

"Ready?" Shade asked.

Maggie nodded, and suddenly, the world around her transformed. Her bedroom became a lush, moonlit forest.

The carpet turned to soft moss under her feet, and her toy chest became a fallen log covered in glowing mushrooms.

"Wow!" Maggie gasped, her eyes wide with wonder.

"This is Shadow Wood," Shade explained. "It's a magical place that only exists in the darkness. Want to explore?"

Hand in hand (or rather, hand in shadow), Maggie and Shade set off into the enchanted forest. They danced with fireflies, slid down moonbeams, and played hide-and-seek with friendly owls.

Maggie had never had so much fun in the dark before!

As they walked along a babbling brook made of starlight,Maggie heard a soft sniffling sound.

"What's that?" she asked.

"Let's find out," said Shade.

They followed the sound to a small clearing where they found a tiny shadow creature crying.

"What's wrong?" Maggie asked gently.

The little shadow looked up, startled. "I'm lost," it whimpered. "I can't find my way home."

Maggie looked at Shade, who nodded encouragingly. "We'll help you," Maggie said, holding out her hand to the little shadow.

Together, the three of them searched Shadow Wood. Maggie was surprised to find that she wasn't scared at all. With Shade by her side, she felt brave and strong.

Finally, they found a cozy shadow burrow where a worried shadow family was waiting. The little shadow creature squealed with delight and ran to its parents.

"Thank you," the shadow family said to Maggie and Shade. "You're welcome in Shadow Wood anytime!"

As they waved goodbye, Maggie yawned. The night's adventures had made her sleepy.

"Time to head back," Shade said softly.

In the blink of an eye, they were back in Maggie’s room. The forest was gone, but the magic of the night remained.

Maggie climbed into bed, a big smile on her face.

"Thank you, Shade," she said. "I'm not scared of the dark anymore."

Shade tucked her in, its shadowy form gentle and comforting.

"I'm always here for you,Maggie. Whenever you feel scared, just remember the wonders we saw tonight."

As Maggie drifted off to sleep, she knew she'd never fear the darkness again. For in the shadows, she had found a true friend.

From that night on, Maggie looked forward to bedtime. Each night brought new adventures with Shade in Shadow Wood.

And even on nights when they stayed in her room, Maggie felt safe and happy, knowing her friendly shadow was always there, watching over her as she slept.

Sweet dreams, Maggie. And remember, sometimes the best friends are found in the most unexpected places – even in the shadows.

The Time-Traveling Teddy: Emily's Midnight Adventure

Emily hugged her favorite teddy bear, Buttons, close as she snuggled under her cozy blanket.

"Goodnight, Buttons," she whispered, giving him an extra squeeze. "I wonder what adventures we'll have in my dreams tonight?"

As Emily drifted off to sleep, something magical happened. Buttons' eyes began to twinkle, and a soft, golden glow surrounded him.

Suddenly, Emily found herself wide awake, sitting up in bed with Buttons by her side.

"Emily," said Buttons in a gentle voice, "are you ready for an adventure?"

Emily's eyes widened with surprise and delight. "Buttons! You can talk!"

The teddy bear chuckled. "Only in your dreams, Emily. And in your dreams, we can go anywhere in history. Where would you like to go tonight?"

Emily thought for a moment. "Oh! Can we see the dinosaurs?"

Buttons nodded, his button eyes sparkling. "Hold on tight!"

With a whoosh and a whirl, Emily's bedroom faded away. When everything came back into focus, Emily and Buttons were standing in a lush, green forest.

Tall ferns swayed in the breeze, and the air was warm and humid.

"Wow!" Emily exclaimed, looking around in wonder. "Are we really in the time of dinosaurs?"

Just then, they heard a thunderous roar. Emily grabbed Buttons tightly as a massive Tyrannosaurus Rex stomped into view.

"Don't worry," Buttons whispered. "We're just watching. It can't see or hurt us."

Emily watched in awe as the T-Rex sniffed the air and then moved on, its huge feet shaking the ground with each step.

"That was amazing!" Emily said. "But also a little scary."

Buttons patted her hand. "It's okay to feel scared sometimes. Being brave doesn't mean you're never afraid. It means doing things even when you are afraid."

Emily nodded, understanding. "Can we see something less scary now?"

"Of course," said Buttons. "How about ancient Egypt?"

With another whoosh, the prehistoric forest disappeared, replaced by the hot, dry air of the Egyptian desert.

Emily and Buttons found themselves standing before an enormous pyramid, still under construction.

"Look at all the people working together," Emily marveled, watching as workers hauled huge stone blocks up ramps.

"Yes," Buttons agreed. "It took many years and thousands of people to build a single pyramid. It shows what humans can achieve when they work together."

Emily watched the scene for a while, fascinated by the ancient tools and techniques.

"It's so different from how we build things today," she observed.

"That's right," said Buttons. "We can learn a lot from studying history. It helps us understand how far we've come and appreciate the knowledge and skills of people who lived long ago."

As the hot sun began to feel uncomfortable, Emily turned to Buttons.

"Can we go somewhere cooler now?"

Buttons nodded, and with another magical whoosh, they found themselves in a grand castle. Snow fell softly outside the windows, and a warm fire crackled in a huge fireplace.

"Welcome to medieval times," Buttons announced. "This is how kings and queens lived hundreds of years ago."

Emily explored the castle, marveling at the tapestries on the walls and the suits of armor standing in the corridors.

In the great hall, musicians played lively tunes as people in colorful clothes danced.

"It looks like so much fun!" Emily said, tapping her foot to the music.

"Life wasn't easy for everyone in these times," Buttons explained gently. "Many people worked very hard and didn't have much. But they still found ways to be happy and celebrate together."

Emily thought about this. "I guess we're lucky to have so many things that make our lives easier now."

"That's right," Buttons agreed. "Each time in history has its own challenges and joys. That's why it's so interesting to learn about different periods."

As they watched the dancing, Emily began to feel sleepy again. She yawned and leaned against Buttons.

"I think it's time to go home," Buttons said softly.

With a final whoosh, Emily found herself back in her own bed, snuggled up with Buttons in her arms.

As she drifted back to sleep, Emily thought about all the amazing things she'd seen. She felt grateful for her comfortable bed, her loving family, and all the wonderful things in her life that people from the past didn't have.

"Thank you, Buttons," she murmured, hugging her teddy bear close. "That was the best adventure ever."

In the soft moonlight, Buttons' button eyes seemed to twinkle once more, as if to say, "You're welcome, Emily. Sweet dreams."

And Emily slept soundly, her dreams filled with dinosaurs, pyramids, and medieval dances, knowing that more adventures with Buttons awaited her in nights to come.

The Cloud Painter

Once upon a time, in a cozy little house on top of a hill, there lived a young girl named Rose. Rose loved to paint more than anything in the world.

Her room was filled with colorful drawings of flowers, animals, and fantastic creatures that sprang from her imagination.

One day, Rose's grandmother gave her a special gift – a set of shimmering paints that seemed to glow with an inner light.

"These are magic paints," her grandmother whispered with a wink. "Use them wisely, and remember, with great power comes great responsibility."

Rose was thrilled with her new paints and couldn't wait to try them out. That night, as the sun set and the sky turned a beautiful shade of pink, Rose set up her easel by the window. She dipped her brush into the silvery paint and began to create.

As she painted, something extraordinary happened. The fluffy white cloud she had drawn began to rise off the paper and float out the window!

Rose gasped in amazement as her painted cloud joined the real clouds in the sky.

Excited by her discovery, Rose painted more clouds – big, puffy ones that looked like cotton candy, and long, wispy ones that streaked across the sky like brushstrokes. Soon, the evening sky was filled with her creations.

The next morning, Rose woke up to find the whole town buzzing with excitement. Everyone was talking about the unusual and beautiful cloud formations they had seen the night before.

Rose smiled to herself, knowing her secret.

Each night after that, Rose would wait until the stars came out, then paint new wonders in the sky. She painted rainbows that shimmered even in the dark, and northern lights that danced above the rooftops.

The townspeople were amazed by the nightly displays, calling them "sky magic."

One evening, feeling particularly creative, Rose decided to paint a gentle rain shower. She mixed blues and grays, adding little droplets with quick strokes of her brush. To her delight, a small rain cloud formed and drifted out the window.

But as she watched, the cloud grew bigger and darker.

Soon, a heavy rainstorm was pouring down on the town. Lightning flashed, and thunder boomed. Rose tried to paint sunshine to make the storm go away, but the magic paints had run out.

She watched anxiously as the storm she had created raged on.

Just when Rose thought things couldn't get any worse, she heard a knock at her door. It was her grandmother.

"I see you've discovered the power of the magic paints," she said gently.

Rose nodded, tears in her eyes. "I didn't mean to cause a storm. I just wanted to make something beautiful."

Her grandmother smiled and took Rose’s hand. "Creating beauty is a wonderful thing, but we must always consider the consequences of our actions. Even the most beautiful rain can cause problems if there's too much of it."

Together, they went to Rose’s easel. Her grandmother showed her how to mix the colors just right to create a soft breeze that would blow the storm clouds away. As they painted, the wind picked up outside, and gradually the storm began to clear.

When the last raincloud had disappeared, Rose's grandmother turned to her.

"You have a wonderful gift, Rose. Your paintings bring joy to everyone who sees them. But remember, with this power comes the responsibility to think about how your creations affect others."

Rose nodded solemnly. From that day on, she continued to paint the sky, but she did so with care and thought. She painted gentle winds on hot days, light dustings of snow for winter fun, and just the right amount of rain to help the flowers grow.

The townspeople never discovered the source of the marvelous sky paintings, but they grew to love the nightly displays. And Rose, watching from her window as people pointed up at her creations with wonder, felt a warm glow of happiness in her heart.

As she grew older, Rose taught other children how to use the magic paints, always reminding them of the importance of painting responsibly.

And so, the little town on the hill became known far and wide as the place where the sky was always filled with wonder and beauty, thanks to the careful brush strokes of Rose, the cloud painter.

The Sock Puppet Theater

In a cozy house on Maple Street, there lived a lonely sock named Donna. She was a cheerful red and white striped sock, but she had lost her pair long ago.

Now, she spent her days at the bottom of the laundry basket, feeling sad and forgotten.

One quiet night, when the house was fast asleep, Donna had an idea. She wriggled her way to the top of the laundry pile and called out, "Friends, I have a plan to brighten our nights!"

A sleepy t-shirt named Tee yawned and asked, "What are you talking about, Donna?"

"We should start a sock puppet theater!" Donna exclaimed. "We can put on shows and entertain ourselves while we wait to be washed!"

A pair of jeans named Jean grumbled, "That's silly. We're just laundry. We can't put on shows."

But a sparkly dress named Glitter twirled excitedly. "Oh, how fun! I've always wanted to be on stage!"

Donna grinned. "See? Glitter's in! Who else wants to join?"

Slowly, more clothes began to show interest. A wooly sweater named Fuzzy offered to be the curtain, and a group of mismatched socks volunteered to be the actors.

"But what about the stories?" asked a curious pillowcase named Fluffy. "What will our plays be about?"

Donna thought for a moment. "We can tell the tales of our adventures in the outside world! Remember when Jean went camping and got covered in mud?"

Jean chuckled. "Oh yes, that was quite a messy trip!"

And so, the Laundry Basket Players were born. Every night, when the house fell silent, the clothes would come to life and put on wonderful shows.

Their first play was "Jean's Muddy Adventure." Donna narrated while two socks, playing Jean and a muddy puddle, acted out the story.

The other clothes watched in delight, giggling quietly so as not to wake the humans.

As the nights went on, the plays became more elaborate. Glitter starred in "The Ballroom Dance Disaster," a hilarious tale about the time she got caught on a door handle during a fancy party.

Tee and Fuzzy teamed up for "The Great Drying Rack Escape," recounting their daring adventure when a gust of wind blew them off the clothesline.

Donna loved every moment. She wasn't lonely anymore, and she had found her talent as a director and storyteller. The laundry basket was filled with laughter and friendship.

One night, as they were preparing for their newest play, "The Case of the Missing Sock" (starring Donna herself), they heard footsteps approaching. Quick as a flash, all the clothes fell silent and still.

The laundry room door creaked open, and in walked Mom, yawning and carrying an armful of dirty clothes. As she dumped the new laundry into the basket, she paused, looking puzzled.

"That's strange," she muttered, picking up Donna. "I could have sworn this sock was at the bottom yesterday. How did it get up here?"

For a heart-stopping moment, Donna thought their secret would be discovered. But then Mom shrugged, dropped her back in the basket, and left the room.

Once the door closed, the clothes let out a collective sigh of relief.

"That was close!" whispered Glitter.

"Maybe we should be more careful," said Jean worriedly.

But Donna just smiled. "Friends, I think we just got inspiration for our next play: 'The Midnight Laundry Mix-Up'!"

The others chuckled softly, and they began planning their new show with excitement.

As the weeks passed, the Laundry Basket Players became the highlight of the clothes' lives.

They looked forward to each performance, and with Donna's encouragement, even the most reluctant members, like Jean, started to enjoy participating.

Donna was happier than she had ever been. She may have lost her pair, but she had gained a whole family of friends.

Every sock, shirt, and pair of pants in the basket knew they could count on each other, no matter how tangled or wrinkled life became.

One day, as Mom was sorting laundry, she picked up Donna and smiled. "You know," she said to herself, "I could have sworn this sock didn't have a pair, but it always seems to end up with the happiest pile of laundry. Maybe there's some laundry magic at work here!"

If only she knew about the nightly performances and the joy that filled her laundry basket when the lights went out.

But that was a secret the Laundry Basket Players would always keep, tucked away like a precious sock in a drawer.

And so, night after night, the plays went on. In the cozy house on Maple Street, a laundry basket full of love, laughter, and friendship sat quietly in the corner, waiting for the sun to set and the next great performance to begin.

Donna, once the loneliest sock in the basket, now fell asleep each night with a smile on her face, dreaming of the next wonderful story she would tell with her dear friends.

In the world of the Laundry Basket Players, every piece of clothing had a part to play, and every night was opening night.

Sofie the Brave Mermaid

Once upon a time, in the shimmering waters of Aquaria, there lived a kind-hearted mermaid named Sofie. With flowing fins of aquamarine and sparkling seashells decorating her long hair, she spent her days exploring the vibrant coral reefs, playing with schools of fish, and collecting treasures from shipwrecks.

But unlike many other mermaids, Sofie was not just curious about her underwater world; she was also enchanted by the tales of the surface world—stories of adventure, bravery, and the beautiful landscapes above the sea.

One stormy night, a wild tempest roared over the ocean, crashing waves against ancient cliffs. Sofie was swimming near the surface when she spotted a ship struggling against the powerful winds.

Its sails flapped wildly like frightened birds, and the ship pitched and rolled in the unforgiving waters. Sofie's heart raced.

"Those sailors need help!" she thought as she swam closer.

Suddenly, a crash boomed, and a massive wave overwhelmed the ship. The vessel began to sink, splintering wood and frightened cries echoing in the chaos. In the frantic scene, Sofie saw a young boy thrown overboard, his arms flailing as he fought to stay afloat.

It was the sailor's apprentice, lost and alone in the raging sea.

Without a second thought, Sofie dove into the turbulent waters. The storm churned around her, but the mermaid was determined. With swift kicks of her powerful tail, she reached the boy just as he began to sink beneath the frothy waves.

"Hold on!" Sofie shouted, wrapping her arms around him.

The young boy, shivering and terrified, looked up at the radiant mermaid.

"Who are you?" he gasped.

“I’m Sofie, and I’m here to help you!” she promised, giving him a reassuring smile.

Then, with all her strength, she propelled them both toward the shore, fighting against the fierce currents.

After what felt like an eternity, Sofie finally reached the sandy beach. Gently, she pulled the boy to safety, collapsing on the shore beside him.

They both gasped for breath, the storm still raging behind them. As the waves crashed dramatically behind them, Sofie turned to the boy. “Are you okay?”

“I think so,” the boy replied, shaking off water and looking up at his savior with wide eyes. “You saved my life! I thought I would drown out there!”

Sofie smiled warmly, her heart lightened by his gratitude.

“I couldn’t just leave you there. What’s your name?”

“I’m Aiden,” he said, looking perplexed. “But my crew... I need to find them!”

The realization struck Sofie like a lightning bolt.

“You need to go back to the spot the ship sank. I can help!”

Aiden nodded, his determination firm. “Yes! Thank you!”

Without hesitation, Sofie took Aiden’s hand and dove into the ocean, the murky waters swirling around them. When they reached the wreck, Sofie helped Aiden find the lifeboats.

“Quick! Grab onto that boat!” she instructed, pointing toward a half-submerged vessel still tethered to the ship.

Aiden held tightly as Sofie used all of her strength to pull the boat towards the shore.

Just as they reached the beach, she heard cries from deeper in the ocean. Sofie quickly swam back to where the other lifeboats were drifting.

One by one, she dragged them to safety, ensuring that each sailor reached the shore where they would be safe from the storm.

Finally, after what felt like hours, Sofie emerged from the waves, the last life boat in tow. The sailors cheered, their spirits lifted by the brave mermaid who had saved them.

“Thank you, Sofie!” Aiden called, beaming with gratitude. “You’re incredible!”

Just then, Aiden’s expression changed. He looked at Sofie with wonder.

“You saved me and my crew, but I still don’t know who you are—truly. I’ve heard tales of mermaids. I thought they were just legends!”

Sofie blushed and flicked her tail bashfully.

“I am just a mermaid who cares for the sea and its people.”

The sailors gathered around, asking questions about life under the sea. In the excitement, Aiden felt a yearning in his heart. He wanted to discover the mysteries of the ocean that Sofie called home.

“Could you show me your world beneath the waves?” he asked, hope shining in his eyes.

Sofie thought for a moment. She could show him the wonders of her underwater realm and share with him the beauty that resided below the surface.

“Yes, I would be happy to show you! But we must wait until dawn. The morning light reveals so much beauty in the sea.”

As the sun began to rise, casting golden rays over the beach, Sofie led Aiden back into the water. With the soft light flickering gently on the waves, Sofie took Aiden’s hand and guided him underwater.

As they descended, the world transformed into a dazzling spectacle of colors and life.

They swam through brilliant coral gardens painted in reds, yellows, and blues, schools of shimmering fish darting around them like living jewels. Sofie pointed out sea turtles gliding gracefully and playful dolphins leaping above the waves.

Aiden's eyes widened in awe as he took in the beauty of the underwater kingdom.

"Look!" Sofie said, motioning toward a sunken ship covered in colorful seaweed and barnacles. "That ship was lost long ago. Come, let's explore it!"

As they swam inside, Aiden discovered treasure chests filled with sparkling stones, ancient artifacts, and forgotten tales that whispered through the currents like soft melodies.

He realized that the ocean was filled with wondrous secrets, just waiting to be uncovered.

"Thank you for showing me this," Aiden said, eyes sparkling with excitement. "It's incredible! I never imagined the world was this beautiful beneath the waves."

But as they swam back up to the surface, Aiden felt a twinge of sadness.

"I am a sailor, and I must return to my crew. But I want to learn more about both worlds."

Sofie smiled, understanding his dilemma.

"You can always come back to visit me. You can bridge both worlds, Aiden. The sea and the sky are both beautiful; you'll be able to explore both."

As they reached the shore, Aiden looked back at Sofie, gratitude filling his heart.

"I promise to return, and I'll tell everyone about your world. You deserve to be known for your bravery and kindness."

With one last splash of her tail, Sofie waved goodbye as Aiden joined his crew, ready to share the stories of adventure and wonder that awaited both above and beneath the sea.

And from that day forward, Aiden became a storyteller, cherishing the friendship of a brave mermaid named Sofie, who taught him that beauty exists in both worlds—whether above the waves or below, every adventure was a treasure worth discovering.

The Whispering Library

In the heart of a sleepy little town stood an old library. Its walls were made of weathered brick, and its windows were always a little dusty. But inside, oh, inside was a world of wonder!

Shelves upon shelves reached up to the ceiling, each one filled with books of every size, color, and story you could imagine.

During the day, the library was quiet. Children would tiptoe through the aisles, picking out their favorite tales.

Adults would browse the shelves, searching for new adventures. And the kindly old librarian, Ms. Paige, would shuffle about, making sure every book was in its proper place.

But at night, when the last patron had left and Ms. Paige had turned out the lights, something magical happened.

As the moon rose high in the sky, casting silver beams through the dusty windows, the books began to stir. First, a gentle rustling, like leaves in a soft wind.

Then, quiet murmurs, growing louder and louder until the whole library was filled with excited whispers.

"It's time!" announced a deep, booming voice.

It belonged to the biggest book in the library, a massive encyclopedia that sat importantly on a special shelf.

Slowly, books began to open. Their pages fluttered, and from between them emerged tiny figures – the characters from each story! They climbed down from their shelves using bookmarks as slides and bits of string as ropes.

In the center of the library, they gathered in a big circle. There was a brave knight in shining armor, a curious little mouse, a grumpy old troll, a beautiful princess, a mischievous pirate, and so many more.

"Who would like to share their story tonight?" asked a wise old owl, who had flown down from a book of fairy tales.

A small, rather worn-out book raised its cover timidly. "M-may I?" it asked in a soft voice.

"Of course!" the owl hooted encouragingly. "Come to the center, little one."

The book shyly made its way to the middle of the circle. As it opened its pages, a gust of wind whooshed out, carrying with it the scent of salt and sea.

Suddenly, everyone found themselves on a sandy beach. Waves crashed against the shore, and seagulls cried overhead.

"This is the story of a little hermit crab named Henry," the book began. "Henry was afraid of the big, wide ocean. He always hid in his shell, too scared to come out and make friends."

As the book spoke, a tiny hermit crab scuttled across the sand. All the characters watched, fascinated, as Henry the hermit crab learned to be brave, make friends with fish and sea stars, and even save a baby turtle.

When the story was finished, everyone clapped and cheered. The beach faded away, and they were back in the library.

"What a wonderful tale!" exclaimed a dictionary, who didn't often get to enjoy stories.

"I never knew the ocean could be so exciting!" said a book about deserts.

The little book glowed with pride. "Thank you," it said. "I've always been a bit shy, like Henry. But sharing my story has made me feel braver."

And so the night went on, with books taking turns to share their stories. There were tales of grand adventures, silly jokes that made everyone giggle, and quiet, cozy stories that made even the most excitable characters feel sleepy.

As the first light of dawn began to creep through the windows, the owl called out, "It's time to return to our shelves, friends. Thank you all for a magical night of stories!"

The characters said their goodbyes and climbed back into their books. The pages closed gently, and soon the library was quiet once more.

When Ms. Paige arrived that morning, she found the library just as she had left it. But if she had looked very closely, she might have noticed that some of the books were sitting a little closer together, like good friends sharing a secret.

So the next time you visit a library, remember: every book has a story to tell, not just on its pages, but in its heart. All you have to do is listen.

Now, close your eyes and dream of the wonderful tales waiting for you on those shelves. Who knows?

Maybe tonight, in your dreams, you'll get to join the magical gathering in the whispering library.

Goodnight, little one. Sweet dreams.

Captain Lily and the Golden Treasure

Once upon a time, in a bustling seaside town, lived a courageous girl named Captain Lily. With her wild, curly hair and a bright red bandana tied around her head, she was known far and wide as the bravest pirate on the seven seas!

Captain Lily didn't sail on just any ship; she commanded the mighty Rainbow Star, a fantastical vessel with sails of every color and a crew of merry animals—her best friends.

There was Finn the clever parrot, who loved to squawk riddles; Bella the plucky dog, who had a nose for adventure; and Ollie the wise old turtle, who told stories of the ocean's secrets.

Together, they sailed the sparkling waters, searching for treasure and excitement.

One glorious morning, as the sun peeked over the horizon, Captain Lily and her crew gathered around a weathered treasure map they'd discovered hidden in an old bottle.

"Look here!" Lily pointed at the map with excitement. "It says that the Golden Treasure of Coral Cove is hidden beneath the waves, guarded by the elusive Sea Serpent!"

Bella wagged her tail. "A treasure hunt! Oh, how thrilling! Can we go, Captain?"

"Of course!" Lily replied, a twinkle in her eye. "Adventure awaits!"

With a hearty cheer, the crew set sail, the Rainbow Star gliding swiftly across the sparkling ocean. As they journeyed, Finn perched on Captain Lily's shoulder, squawking riddles to keep the spirit high.

"What has a heart that doesn't beat?" he asked, and the crew racked their brains until Bella shouted, "An artichoke!"

With laughter echoing across the waves, they sailed until they reached the mysterious Coral Cove. The water shimmered in vibrant hues of blue and green, with beautiful coral reefs dancing beneath the surface.

"Look!" Ollie pointed with his flipper. "I see a glittering light over there!"

Captain Lily squinted toward the glow. "That must be the Golden Treasure!"

As they approached the shimmering light, they suddenly found themselves face-to-face with the Sea Serpent! It was a magnificent creature with shining scales that reflected the sun like diamonds.

"Who dares disturb my waters?" the Serpent boomed, its voice booming like thunder.

Lily swallowed her fear and stood tall. "I am Captain Lily, and I've come to seek the Golden Treasure. We mean no harm; we only wish to explore!"

The Sea Serpent's eyes sparkled with curiosity.

"Treasure seekers, huh? Many have tried to claim the treasure, but it belongs to the ocean. You must prove your worth."

"What do we need to do?" Lily asked bravely.

"To earn the treasure, you must solve three challenges," boomed the Sea Serpent. "If you succeed, the treasure is yours!"

"Our adventure has just begun!" Lily cheered, and her crew celebrated.

The first challenge was a riddle. The Sea Serpent asked, "I am not alive but I can grow; I don't have lungs but I need air. What am I?"

Finn's feathers ruffled with excitement.

"It's fire!" he squawked.

The Sea Serpent nodded, impressed. "Well done, brave crew!"

For the second challenge, they had to collect beautiful sea shells scattered along the shore. Bella dashed around, sniffing out the most colorful shells, while Lily helped collect them in a big net.

When they returned, the Sea Serpent smiled. “You truly have an eye for beauty!”

For the final challenge, the Sea Serpent tested their teamwork. “You must sing a song together that honors the ocean!”

With no time to spare, the crew huddled together and sang a joyful tune about the waves, the stars, and the treasures of friendship.

The Sea Serpent listened closely, swaying to the melody, and when they finished, it smiled a wide, toothy grin.

“You have proven yourselves worthy, Captain Lily and your crew! The Golden Treasure is yours!”

With a majestic wave of its tail, the Sea Serpent revealed a hidden cave beneath the coral, filled with gold coins, sparkling jewels, and magical trinkets.

Captain Lily and her crew cheered with delight!

"We did it!" Lily exclaimed, dancing with Bella and Finn. Ollie clapped his flippers proudly.

But then, Lily paused.

"Wait! We should share our treasure with the townsfolk! They've helped us pursue our dreams."

The Sea Serpent nodded approvingly. "A true captain knows the importance of sharing."

So, with the Rainbow Star filled with treasures, they set sail back to the town, greeted with widening eyes and endless cheers.

Lily and her crew shared the golden coins and sparkling jewels, bringing joy to everyone.

As the sun dipped below the horizon, painting the sky with orange and pink, Captain Lily smiled, knowing that the greatest treasure of all was the friendship they had built and the adventures that lay ahead.

And from that day forward, Captain Lily and her crew continued to sail together, discovering new wonders and sharing stories of bravery, kindness, and the joy of adventure.

Stella's Stardust Adventure

Once upon a time, in a quiet little town, there lived a curious girl named Stella. Stella was no ordinary girl; she dreamed of becoming an astronaut!

Every night, she would stare up at the twinkling stars, imagining herself zipping through the galaxy in a shiny spaceship. She read countless books about planets, moons, and brave astronauts who floated among the stars.

Her heart raced with excitement at the thought of the adventures waiting for her in space.

One fateful evening, as Stella was laying in bed, she spotted a shooting star streaking across the sky.

“Wow!” she gasped, barely able to contain her excitement. “I wish I could visit the stars!”

Little did she know, her wish was about to come true!

With a whoosh! A flicker of sparkling stardust filled her bedroom, and Stella’s eyes widened in surprise. Before her stood a shimmering figure made of starlight.

“Hello, Stella! I’m Nova, the Star Fairy! You wished to see the stars, and I’m here to take you on a magical adventure!”

Stella jumped up, her heart fluttering.

“Really? This is amazing! I can’t wait!”

She quickly grabbed her favorite stuffed rocket ship, Mr. Rocket, and together they followed Nova into the glowing stardust.

In an instant, they were aboard Nova's ship, the Stardust Voyager. It was dazzling, filled with twinkling lights and buttons that beeped happily.

Nova showed Stella how to strap into her seat.

“Hold on tight! We’re going to blast off!”

With a count of three, Nova pushed a shiny red button, and the ship roared to life.

“Three, two, one... Blast off!”

Stella squealed with delight as the Stardust Voyager shot through the night sky, leaving a trail of glittering stardust behind.

As they soared higher and higher, the ground below grew smaller until the town looked like a tiny dot. Stella pressed her nose against the window, marveling at the beauty of the world below.

Soon they broke through the clouds and into the vastness of space, where stars sparkled like diamonds against the dark canvas of the universe.

Their first stop was the Moon. Nova guided the ship gently to land on the soft, silvery surface.

“Welcome to Moonland!” she cheered.

Stella couldn't believe her eyes; the Moon was a magical place with bouncy crater hills and shimmering moon dust.

Stella hopped out of the ship and leaped joyfully across the Moon’s surface.

“This is so much fun!” She giggled as she bounced higher and higher, making moon angels in the glimmering dust.

Nova laughed, joining in on the fun, and soon they were leaping and twirling like the stars themselves.

After playtime on the Moon, Nova and Stella climbed back aboard the Stardust Voyager.

“Now, let’s visit Saturn!” Nova said excitedly.

With another press of the shiny red button, they soared toward the rings of the magnificent planet.

When they arrived, Stella's eyes widened in amazement. Saturn was stunning, with its swirling colors and majestic rings that sparkled in the sunlight.

“Can we go explore the rings?” Stella asked eagerly.

“Of course!” replied Nova.

With a wave of her hand, the Stardust Voyager hovered close to the rings, and they put on special space suits to float outside. They glided through the sparkling rings, catching glimmers of ice and rock, laughing as they swirled around each other.

Stella reached out her hand, catching a handful of stardust.

“This is the best adventure ever!” she shouted, her heart soaring with happiness.

After their thrilling journey around Saturn, Stella and Nova continued their adventure, visiting vibrant stars that danced in the sky and comets that zipped past with shiny tails.

Each new destination was more exciting than the last, and Stella couldn’t believe how much magic there was in the universe.

As the night began to fade, Nova glanced at Stella with a gentle smile.

"It's time to return home now, Stella. You have many dreams awaiting you on Earth, and the stars will always be here to inspire you."

With a bittersweet feeling, Stella nodded, knowing her adventure must come to an end.

"I'll never forget this!" Stella said. "Thank you, Nova!"

With one last amazing leap into the Stardust Voyager, the ship zoomed back toward Earth, and Stella could see her little town shining brightly below. As they landed softly in her room, the stardust sparkled all around them.

"Remember, Stella," Nova said, "the universe is vast, and your dreams can take you anywhere. Always reach for the stars!"

Stella hugged Mr. Rocket tight, her heart full of joy.

"I will!" she promised.

As the stardust faded and Nova disappeared into the night, Stella climbed into bed, her eyes twinkling like the stars themselves.

She drifted off to sleep, dreaming of Saturn's rings, moon dust, and all the adventures that awaited her among the stars.

From that day on, every time Stella looked up at the night sky, she smiled, knowing that one day, she would return to the stars.

Mia's Magical Soccer Game

Once upon a time in the sunny town of Willow Creek, there lived a spirited girl named Mia. Mia had golden hair that bounced with every step she took and a heart full of dreams.

She loved playing soccer more than anything else in the world. Every day after school, she would race to the park, lace up her shimmering pink cleats, and practice her dribbling, passing, and shooting skills.

Mia was part of the Willow Creek Unicorns, a spirited girls' soccer team with bright blue uniforms and a sparkling unicorn logo. They practiced every Tuesday and Thursday, and every Saturday, they played against other teams in the league.

Mia dreamed of scoring the winning goal in the championship game, which was just around the corner.

One sunny Saturday morning, Mia and her teammates gathered at the park for a big practice. The air was filled with excitement as they ran drills and cheered each other on. Coach Sarah gathered the girls together.

“Unicorns,” she said, “the championship game is next week, and I know you’ve all been practicing hard. Remember, teamwork and supporting each other is what makes us special!”

Mia nodded enthusiastically. She loved her teammates: Lisa, who was quick and clever; Ava, whose strong kicks could send the ball soaring; and Sharin, the best goalie around.

Together, they were a force to be reckoned with!

As they practiced, Mia noticed a dazzling shimmer in the air. Suddenly, out of nowhere, a small, sparkly figure appeared!

It was Zara, the Soccer Fairy! She had glimmering wings and a magical smile.

“Hello, Mia! I’ve come to help you and your team in the championship game!” she said with a twinkle in her eyes.

Mia gasped in disbelief. “A real fairy? What can you do to help us?”

Zara giggled and waved her wand, drawing colorful patterns in the air.

“I can inspire you! Together, we’ll unlock your true potential.” Zara said. “When the time comes, trust your heart and remember the magic of teamwork.”

With a sprinkle of stardust, Zara faded away, leaving Mia wide-eyed with wonder.

“Did that really happen?” Mia whispered to herself, feeling a mix of excitement and curiosity.

The days passed quickly, and soon the day of the championship arrived. The sun was bright, and butterflies danced in the sky as Mia and her friends gathered on the field.

Other teams were warming up, and the air buzzed with anticipation. Mia's heart raced as she looked at the shiny trophy waiting on a table nearby.

As the game began, the Unicorns faced a tough opponent, the Thunderbolts, known for their speed and skill. Mia felt a flutter in her stomach as the referee blew the whistle.

The sound echoed like a call to action, and the game kicked off!

The Thunderbolts shot forward, quickly moving the ball and scoring the first goal. The crowd erupted into cheers, but Mia and her teammates didn't give up.

They rallied together on the field.

“We can do this! Unicorns together!” yelled Lisa, as they gathered around Coach Sarah for a quick pep talk.

As the game progressed, the girls supported one another, passing the ball and cheering each other on. Mia felt more confident and focused, remembering what Zara the Soccer Fairy had said about teamwork.

Ava sprinted down the field, dodging a Thunderbolt defender.

“Mia! Over here!” she called. Mia dashed toward her friend, ready to receive the pass. The ball rolled toward her, and with one swift motion, she kicked it toward the goal—missed!

But instead of feeling disappointed, she shook it off.

“Okay, I’ll try again!” she thought, determined to make her team proud. The Unicorns kept pushing forward, working together.

With just a few minutes left on the clock, the score was tied 1-1. The pressure was building, and everyone could feel it. Then Mia spotted the perfect opportunity.

"Now's my chance," she whispered.

Lisa passed the ball to Mia, who took a deep breath and remembered Zara's words. With purpose, she dribbled the ball with skill and grace, weaving past defenders.

Time felt like it was slowing down as she approached the goal. The goalie from the Thunderbolts was ready, but Mia knew just what to do.

With all her might, Mia took a powerful shot! The ball soared through the air, gliding past the goalkeeper and into the back of the net!

GOOOOOOOOOOOAL!

The crowd erupted in cheers, and her teammates rushed to embrace her.

Mia’s heart soared with joy. They had done it—the Unicorns were champions! As the referee blew the final whistle, Zara the Soccer Fairy appeared once more, sparkling like the stars.

“You showed incredible teamwork and heart today, Mia! Always believe in yourselves and each other.”

With the shining trophy held high, Mia beamed with pride. She knew this wasn’t just about winning; it was about friendship, hard work, and the magic they shared.

That night, as she lay in bed, Mia whispered, "Thank you, Fairy Zara," before drifting off to sleep with dreams of new adventures, glittering goals, and a world where anything felt possible.

Naomi and the Great Swamp Showdown

In the peaceful town of Maryville, there lived a kind-hearted girl named Naomi. With her bright smile and boundless enthusiasm, she loved exploring the world around her, especially the lush green fields and the magical swamps nearby.

Naomi spent her days helping her neighbors, collecting litter in the park, and even planting flowers.

One fateful day, as she wandered near the swamp, she noticed something odd. The once-clear waters were murky and filled with trash.

The chirping frogs were silent, the dragonflies had disappeared, and a strange smell hung in the air. Concerned, Naomi approached the swamp's edge.

Suddenly, from the depths of the swamp, a loud crashing noise erupted. Made of mud, sludge, and rubbish, a giant bog monster rose from the water!

His enormous, gooey body shimmered with plastic and old junk, and his glowing yellow eyes looked both sad and angry.

“What have you done to my swamp?” Naomi gasped. She could see the monster was hurt, not just angry.

“I am the Guardian of this swamp!” the monster roared, splattering mud everywhere. “But I’ve been awakened by the pollution that now fills my home! I can’t protect the swamp, and it’s dying because of all the trash!”

Naomi felt a pang of compassion for the monster. She understood that his rage came from a place of sadness.

“I want to help you!” she called out bravely. “Together, we can restore your home!”

The bog monster paused, surprised. “You would help someone like me? I’m just a monster now.”

"No," Naomi replied, shaking her head. "You're not just a monster. You're a guardian! Every creature deserves to be protected."

As the words left her lips, Naomi felt a surge of energy course through her. A soft, glowing light enveloped her, and in that moment, she realized she had been granted magical powers.

She could not only understand the language of nature but could also summon the elements of the earth to aid her.

"Alright, let's show everyone how important it is to care for this swamp!" Naomi declared, her heart pounding with excitement. "Together, we can save it!"

The bog monster's eyes brightened.

"I can help you gather the creatures of the swamp. They can join us in fighting against the pollution!"

With a shout, Naomi exclaimed, "Let's do it!"

She raised her hands in the air, and with a wave of her arms, a flurry of starlight swirled around her. She called upon the local animals—frogs, birds, and even the shy raccoons—all eager to respond to her plea.

As the creatures gathered, Naomi devised a plan.

"We'll have a Swamp Clean-Up Day! We can collect all the garbage and make this place beautiful again. And then, we can show the town why it's essential to protect our environment!"

The bog monster nodded enthusiastically, his muddy exterior shimmering with hope. "I will use my strength to help us lift heavier objects. Let's get to work!"

As the sun began to rise, the townspeople watched in surprise as Naomi and her new friends—the bog monster and the creatures of the swamp—marched together into town, armed with brooms, nets, and garbage bags.

Naomi stood tall, addressing the crowd. "We need your help! The swamp is suffering from pollution, and we can't let it die!"

Some townspeople were skeptical, while others wondered what they could do. Seeing the courage on Naomi's face and the determination in the bog monster's eyes, a few brave kids stepped forward.

"We'll help!" they shouted.

As the group spread the word, more and more townsfolk joined. They gathered supplies, rallied together, and within hours, the Swamp Clean-Up Day had begun. Naomi and the bog monster led the way, encouraging everyone to pick up litter, pour out pollution, and recycle whatever they could.

Working together, the community collected bag after bag of trash, each piece leaving the swamp cleaner and brighter. The bog monster used his strength to lift heavy debris, while Naomi inspired everyone with her kind spirit and energy.

As they cleaned, Naomi taught the townsfolk why protecting the environment was vital. Together, they planted flowers, hung signs about caring for the earth, and spread awareness about pollution.

Finally, after hours of hard work, they looked around in awe. The swamp sparkled once again, with life returning all around—frogs croaked happily, dragonflies danced in the air, and even the sun shone brighter.

“You’ve saved my home!” the bog monster bellowed joyfully, his heart brimming with gratitude.

The townsfolk cheered, realizing that they could be guardians of the earth too.

From that day forward, Naomi became the hero of Maryville and an advocate for the environment. Working side by side with her new friend, the bog monster, she taught others the power of caring for nature.

Every week, they held clean-up days and celebrated the beauty of their surroundings.

As night fell, Naomi gazed at the stars twinkling above, knowing her heart was filled with the brightest light of all—the light of friendship and kindness.

And from that day on, whenever anyone in Maryville looked at the beautiful swamp, they remembered the incredible adventure of Naomi and the bog monster and how they had saved the day together.

Penny and the Magic Quilt

In the quaint town of Petal Grove, there lived a curious girl named Penny. With bright, inquisitive eyes and a heart filled with dreams, Penny loved exploring her world, especially the attic of her grandmother's old house. It was a treasure trove of memories and mysteries, and every time she entered, she imagined the adventures that awaited her.

One rainy afternoon, stuck indoors, Penny visited her grandmother's cozy home. The inviting aroma of freshly baked cookies wafted through the air, making her smile.

After enjoying a cookie (or two), she couldn't resist the urge to venture into the attic.

As Penny climbed the creaky wooden ladder, the door creaked open to a dimly lit room filled with dust-covered trunks and old furniture. But then she noticed it—a patchwork quilt adorned with vibrant colors and intricate designs, draped over a trunk in the center of the room.

Each square depicted a different woman from history, each with a story to tell.

“What a beautiful quilt!” Penny whispered, tracing her fingers over the delicate stitches.

Wondering about the stories behind it, she gently pulled it down, and as she did, a soft glow began to radiate from the quilt.

“Oh, that quilt holds magic!” her grandmother said, appearing behind her. “Legend has it that it can transport you to different times where you can meet remarkable women in history and learn from their lives.”

Penny's eyes sparkled with excitement. “Can I really go there?”

“Only if your heart is true and your intentions are kind,” her grandmother replied. “Just lay under the quilt and wish to go.”

Heart racing with anticipation, Penny climbed beneath the quilt, snuggling into its warmth. “I want to meet the amazing women of history!” she whispered.

In a flash, the attic around her vanished, and she found herself standing in a bustling marketplace, filled with colorful stalls and lively chatter. Penny blinked in awe when she noticed a regal-looking woman with a golden headdress and a commanding presence.

“Welcome! I am Cleopatra, the Queen of Egypt!” she announced, her voice ringing confidently through the air.

“Wow, Cleopatra! What were your greatest achievements?” Penny asked, fascinated.

Cleopatra smiled warmly, her eyes shining with wisdom. “I united my people and strengthened my kingdom through alliances. I fought fiercely for my country and sought knowledge. Remember, always use your voice to uplift those around you!”

Feeling inspired by Cleopatra’s bravery, Penny thanked her and lay beneath the quilt again, eager for the next journey.

With another whoosh, Penny opened her eyes to a dimly lit laboratory filled with bubbling beakers and books stacked high. A young woman with wild curly hair and bright eyes was busy conducting experiments.

“Hello! I am Marie Curie,” she said, adjusting her glasses. “I’m currently studying radioactivity to find cures for illnesses.”

“I’ve heard of you!” Penny exclaimed. “You were the first woman to win a Nobel Prize! What motivated you?”

Marie smiled warmly. “Curiosity and a desire to help people. Science is a path of discovery, and your curiosity can lead to great breakthroughs. Don’t let anyone tell you that you cannot achieve your dreams.”

Feeling invigorated by Marie’s determination, Penny closed her eyes once more, ready for the next adventure.

This time, she found herself in an art studio filled with canvases and paint splatters everywhere. A passionate woman was painting with vibrant colors, her palette exploding with creativity.

“Greetings! I am Frida Kahlo,” she said, her bright eyes shining. “Art is my way of expressing my life and my pain.”

Penny admired Frida’s work and asked, “What advice do you have for a girl who loves to create?”

Frida chuckled softly, “Embrace your uniqueness and share your story through your art. Your experiences shape who you are, so let your creativity flow!”

With newfound inspiration from Frida, Penny returned to the quilt, eager to discover more.

Next, she found herself in a crowded meeting room where women were gathered, passionately advocating for their rights. One woman stood in front, speaking confidently.

"I am Susan B. Anthony," she declared. "I am fighting for women's suffrage—the right for women to vote!"

"How did you keep your courage?" Penny asked, captivated by Susan's resolve.

Susan replied firmly, "We must stand up for justice, even when it's difficult. Change takes time, but with perseverance and unity, we can make a difference."

Feeling the weight of Susan's words, Penny closed her eyes yet again, ready for more wisdom.

Suddenly, she was in a brightly lit office filled with papers and typewriters. A woman with a bright smile was busy at her desk, writing furiously.

"Hello! I'm Eleanor Roosevelt," she greeted. "I believe in human rights and equality for all people."

“What was your greatest achievement?” Penny inquired eagerly.

Eleanor smiled proudly. “I worked to help others and advocated for the rights of women and African Americans. It’s important to be the voice for those who cannot speak for themselves.”

Inspired by her words, Penny wished to continue and found herself in a beautiful garden filled with flowers of every kind. A woman in a sun hat bent over a patch of soil.

“Greetings! I am Wangari Maathai,” she said, her voice warm and welcoming. “I founded the Green Belt Movement to promote environmental conservation and women’s rights in Kenya.”

“What can I do to help the environment?” Penny asked earnestly.

“Plant a tree, conserve water, and always advocate for nature,” Wangari encouraged. “Each small action adds up to a big change.”

Feeling empowered, Penny thanked Wangari and laid down under the quilt once more, absorbing everything she learned.

With another twinkle, she found herself on a bustling stage, where a woman with fierce determination spoke passionately about education.

“I am Malala Yousafzai,” she introduced herself. “I fight for girls’ education around the world.”

Penny gasped in awe. “You’re the youngest Nobel Prize laureate! What made you so brave?”

Malala replied with a smile, “When you stand up for what you believe, you empower others to do the same. Education is a powerful tool; never take it for granted.”

Carrying a heart full of inspiration, Penny laid down under the quilt again, eagerly waiting for her next experience.

This time, she found herself in a vast library filled with books and scrolls. A woman wearing a trench coat and glasses was surrounded by stacks of papers and a typewriter.

“Hello! I’m Harriet Tubman,” she said with a kind smile. “I helped free many enslaved people through the Underground Railroad.”

Penny’s eyes widened. “That’s incredible! How did you manage such bravery?”

Harriet beamed proudly. “I believed in freedom for all and risked my life to help others escape. If you have a cause you believe in, fight for it.”

Feeling a rush of admiration, Penny thanked Harriet and closed her eyes for one last journey.

With a final whoosh, she found herself in a room filled with sewing machines. A woman with a headscarf was stitching beautiful fabrics.

“I am Rosa Parks,” she said. “I stood up for civil rights and sparked the movement that changed our nation.”

“What did it take to refuse to give up your seat?” Penny asked in awe.

“It took courage and a deep sense of justice,” Rosa replied. “When you believe in something, hold your ground. Your actions can inspire many others.”

Penny felt the fire of determination ignite within her. As she closed her eyes one last time, she returned to her grandmother’s attic.

With the cozy quilt wrapped around her, Penny felt profoundly changed. The stories of these incredible women resonated within her, inspiring her to share her voice and dreams with the world.

She rushed down the ladder, excitement bubbling inside her.

“Grandma! I learned so much! I met Cleopatra, Marie Curie, Frida Kahlo, Susan B. Anthony, Eleanor Roosevelt, Wangari Maathai, Malala Yousafzai, Harriet Tubman, and Rosa Parks!

They each taught me about bravery, creativity, equality, and empowerment!"

Her grandmother smiled, her eyes shining with pride.

"Each of those women made a difference in the world, just like you can, Penny. The quilt has magic because it carries the stories of those who dared to dream and act. You have the same potential inside you."

From that day forward, Penny embraced her role as a storyteller and advocate for change in her community.

Inspired by the incredible women she had met, she organized events at school where her classmates could share stories of strong women, create art projects, and work on community service together.

She planted trees in the town park, created a club for girls to explore science and art, and encouraged everyone to stand up for justice. The magic quilt not only transported her to breathtaking moments in history but ignited the flame of inspiration within her heart.

And so, with each new adventure, Penny continued to pave her path, always remembering the remarkable women who came before her and the difference she could make in her own extraordinary journey.

Sherie and the Case of the Missing Apple Pie

Once upon a time in the quaint little town of Maplewood, there lived a brilliant 9-year-old girl named Sherie. With her wild chestnut curls, bright green eyes, and a knack for solving mysteries, Sherie was the town's youngest—and best—detective. She loved nothing more than donning her trusty detective hat, grabbing her magnifying glass, and diving into the latest case that could be found.

One sunny Saturday morning, as the birds chirped merrily outside her window, Sherie was busy organizing her detective notebook. “Alright, what’s next?” she mused, flipping through the pages filled with sketches and notes about her past cases. As she sipped her hot chocolate, a loud knock resounded at her door.

“Sherie! Sherie! You have to come quick!” It was Emma, her best friend, bursting into the room with excitement. Her cheeks were flushed, and her eyes sparkled with urgency.

“What’s wrong, Emma?” Sherie asked, setting her mug down and focusing all her attention on her friend.

“It’s Ms. Thompson! She baked her famous apple pie for the town fair, but it’s gone missing!” Emma exclaimed, her voice a mix of disbelief and worry.

Sherie’s eyes widened. “The apple pie? But that’s the highlight of the fair! Let’s go solve this mystery!”

They quickly dashed to Ms. Thompson’s house, which was just a few blocks away. The sweet aroma of baked goods wafted through the air, mixing with the crisp scent of fall leaves. When they arrived at the front door, Ms. Thompson was waiting, her apron dusted with flour and her face creased with concern.

“Oh, thank goodness you’re here, Sherie!” Ms. Thompson exclaimed. “I prepared my famous apple pie this morning, but when I went to cool it on the window ledge, it vanished! I have no idea what happened!”

“Don’t worry, Ms. Thompson. I’ll find your pie!” Sherie declared confidently, her detective instinct kicking in. She pulled out her notebook and began scribbling notes.

“Was there anyone else around when you set the pie outside?” Sherie asked as she walked over to the window.

“Well, the usual neighborhood kids were playing in the yard,” Ms. Thompson said, scratching her head. “And I saw Mr. Hargrove tending to his garden next door, but I didn’t think much of it. It was all so quiet!”

“Quiet can often be suspicious,” Sherie mumbled thoughtfully. “Emma, let’s talk to the neighborhood kids first!”

Sherie and Emma trotted over to the nearby playground, where a small group of children was gathered around the swing set.

“Hey, everyone! Did you see anything unusual around Ms. Thompson’s house today?” Sherie asked, her hands on her hips.

The kids turned to her, curiosity sparkling in their eyes. “Nope, but we heard a weird noise just before she said the pie went missing!” piped up Jake, a boy with messy hair and a cheeky grin.

“We heard a ‘whoosh’ sound, like something zooming by,” added Lily, another friend from school.

“A ‘whoosh’ sound?” Sherie wrote it down in her notebook. “Interesting! Did anyone see anything that could have made that sound?”

“Not really,” Jake replied, looking puzzled. “But I did see a black cat running really fast after that weird noise.”

“A cat, huh?” Sherie murmured, tapping her chin. “Let’s find that cat, Emma!”

The girls followed the path the children had indicated, leading them into Ms. Thompson’s backyard, where they spotted the neighbor's black cat, Shadow, lounging on the garden fence. She was a fluffy feline with a shiny coat that glimmered in the sunlight.

“Hey, Shadow! Have you seen anything unusual?” Emma called out, bending down to pet the cat gently. Shadow looked up lazily but didn’t seem interested in responding.

Sherie searched the garden but found no physical clues. Just as she was about to give up on the cat, she noticed a set of muddy paw prints leading away from the garden gate. “Look, Emma! Paw prints!” she exclaimed, rushing over to examine them.

“Do you think Shadow could have stolen the pie?” Emma asked.

“Not a chance. She’s not that sneaky,” Sherie replied, grinning. “But these prints might lead us to someone who is!”

Following the paw prints, the girls trekked down the path until they ended up at the corner of Maplewood Street, where they found themselves in front of Mr. Hargrove's house. Mr.

Hargrove was a friendly old man who loved growing vegetables and flowers in his garden.

“Mr. Hargrove, can we ask you a quick question?” Sherie called out.

“Of course, Sherie!” he replied, wiping his hands on his gardening apron. “What brings you here?”

“We’re trying to find Ms. Thompson’s missing apple pie. Did you see anything suspicious?” Sherie inquired, looking him straight in the eye.

Mr. Hargrove scratched his chin, his brow furrowed in thought. “Well, I didn’t see much, but I heard a rustling sound near the fence just a few moments after I noticed Shadow disappear. It was odd, but I didn’t think much of it.”

“Did you see anyone else?” Emma chimed in.

“No, just the usual birds and bees,” he said, shrugging. “But I did catch a glimpse of a raccoon running across the yard. It looked rather hungry.”

"A raccoon, huh?" Sherie noted in her notebook. "Thank you, Mr. Hargrove! We may need to keep an eye out for raccoons."

They left Mr. Hargrove's garden and headed towards a small wooded area nearby. The sun was beginning to set, painting the sky in shades of pink and orange. They had to hurry before darkness fell.

"I think we should look for tiny leftovers or clues the raccoon might have left behind," suggested Emma.

As they searched the area, they found little bits of crumbs scattered on the ground. Sherie's eyes lit up. "These look like crust pieces! Do you think the raccoon could have gotten to the pie?"

Just then, a rustling sound caught their attention, and out from the bushes dashed a small raccoon! The curious little creature was sniffing the air, eyes sparkling with mischief.

"There he is!" exclaimed Emma. "Mr. Raccoon!"

“Hey there, little buddy!” Sherie called out, trying to approach it slowly. The raccoon paused, seemingly in a dilemma between running away and sticking around for some exciting attention.

“Look! He has something in his paws!” Emma noted, pointing.

The raccoon was clutching a half-eaten slice of apple pie cradled in his little paws—a slice that looked just like Ms. Thompson’s!

“Gotcha!” cried Sherie, raising her magnifying glass triumphantly. “This little thief must have snuck into the yard!”

The raccoon froze, the pie slice still clutched in its paws. He stared at the girls, wide-eyed. Sherie smiled, “We’re not mad, buddy. It seems you just wanted a tasty snack.”

Seeing that the raccoon was harmless, Sherie slowly extended her hand. “Can you show us where you found the rest of the pie?”

With a blink, the raccoon took off down the path, looking back as if to say, “Follow me!” Sherie and Emma ran after him, passing through the trees until they reached a shady clearing.

To their surprise, the remnants of the apple pie lay scattered on the ground, surrounded by colorful autumn leaves. The raccoon had clearly enjoyed the pie feast!

“Wow! He really did steal it!” Emma laughed, realizing that the mystery was finally solved.

“But now we need to clean this up and get the word to Ms. Thompson before the fair starts!” Sherie exclaimed, her detective spirit rekindled.

With teamwork, they carefully collected the remains of the pie, making sure to tidy up the area around the clearing. Then they hurried back towards town, the raccoon waddling behind them.

When they reached Ms. Thompson’s house, the fair was just beginning. The air was filled with laughter and the sweet smell of baked goods.

"Ms. Thompson!" Sherie called, waving her hands excitedly.

Ms. Thompson turned, her expression instantly shifting to concern. "Have you found my pie? I was so worried!"

"Well, we found this little guy," Sherie said, pointing at the raccoon, who looked particularly pleased with himself. "He may have taken it into the woods."

Ms. Thompson sighed, giggling when she saw the raccoon. "Oh, that cheeky little rascal has been around all week! I should have known!"

The townsfolk around them laughed, and Ms. Thompson turned to Sherie and Emma. "Thank you, dear detectives! You solved the case of the missing apple pie!"

With smiles bright as the setting sun, Sherie and Emma beamed with pride. They had cracked the mystery, bringing the town together with laughter and sharing the story of Mr. Raccoon's mischievous antics.

As the sun dipped below the horizon and the twinkling lights of the fair illuminated the night, Sherie realized that solving mysteries together made adventures even more special.

Side by side with her best friend, they celebrated not only the return of the missing pie but the joy of friendship and teamwork, waiting for the next mystery to unfold.

Sandi the Space Explorer

Once upon a time, in the sunny town of Brightview, there lived an 11-year-old girl named Sandi. She was not your typical girl; Sandi was a brilliant scientist!

While most kids her age played on the playground or traded snacks, Sandi loved to spend her time in her cozy workshop, where she conducted her own experiments, built fantastic inventions, and dreamed about exploring outer space.

But sometimes, Sandi felt a little out of place. The other kids would say her ideas were "too strange" or "too nerdy," leaving her feeling lonely.

One sunny afternoon, everything changed. There was a knock on Sandi's door. When she opened it, standing there was a tall man in a white lab coat.

“Hello, Sandi! I’m Dr. Wilson, and I’m here on behalf of the National Space Agency. We need your help!”

Sandi’s eyes widened. “You need my help? With what?”

“We’re planning a mission to Mars,” he said, excitement shining in his eyes. “But we’re having some problems getting the rocket ship ready. We heard you’re a genius, and we believe you can help us figure it out!”

“Of course!” Sandi exclaimed, her heart racing with enthusiasm. “I’d love to help!”

They hurried to the nearby Brightview Science Center, where the best scientists in the world were gathered. The room was bustling with excitement, blueprints scattered across tables and models of rockets hanging from the ceiling.

Sandi quickly joined the team, looking at the messy notes, calculations, and sketches.

“This rocket needs to achieve the right speed and angle to reach Mars,” Dr. Wilson said. “We just can’t seem to get it right.”

Sandi analyzed the notes carefully. After a few minutes of thinking, she pointed out a mistake in the calculations for the fuel.

“If we adjust the fuel flow rate here and increase the thrust during launch, it should work perfectly!” she exclaimed.

The scientists buzzed with excitement.

“Brilliant, Sandi! This could change everything!” Dr. Wilson said, clapping her on the back.

Over the next few weeks, Sandi dedicated herself to the mission, solving problems and developing ideas. Everyone was impressed by her ingenuity and creativity.

Then, the day came for the big launch, and Sandi was overjoyed to be invited to fly on the first Mars mission, making her the youngest astronaut ever!

“It’s what I’ve always dreamed of!” Sandi told her mom, who was equally excited but a little worried.

“But just remember,”Mom said “Only if I can go too!”

“Of course, Mom!” Sandi agreed. They both laughed and hugged, thrilled about their new adventure together.

On launch day, the atmosphere was electric. Sandi stood in her space suit, heart thumping as the countdown began.

“Five... four... three... two... one… Blast off!”

The rocket, named the Starlight Voyager, roared to life, shaking with power as it shot into the sky.

As they traveled through space, Sandi gazed out the window in awe, watching Earth shrink into a blue marble far away.

But two weeks into their journey, disaster struck.

“Uh-oh!” Joe, one of the other astronauts, shouted from the cockpit. “We’ve lost our navigation system! We’re drifting off course!”

The crew scrambled, trying to regain control of the ship, but panic began to set in. Dr. Wilson looked worried.

“We have to redirect ourselves fast, or we could miss Mars altogether!” He shouted in a panic.

Sandi’s mind raced.

“Wait!” she shouted, trying to get everyone’s attention. “I can help!”

With her calm, confident demeanor, the crew looked at Sandi, eager for a solution.

“Okay, Sandi, what do you suggest?” Dr. Wilson asked.

“We need to use the emergency landing manual,” Sandi explained, “Let's calculate our trajectory using the stars as reference points!”

She grabbed a piece of paper and began scribbling calculations quickly. Sandi remembered how she learned about constellations during her science club meetings.

Using the window as a guide, she pointed out stars that would help them realign their course.

“Joe, adjust the thrusters to aim at the North Star,” she instructed. “That should help us stabilize and steer back on course.”

With everyone working together, they followed Sandi’s directions. The ship rumbled as they made the necessary adjustments.

“Thrusters engaged!” Joe exclaimed, and the crew felt a jolt as the rocket steadied.

Sandi held her breath. Would it work? The ship gradually regained stability, and they could see the stars spinning into a proper alignment.

A wave of relief washed over Sandi when Dr. Wilson smiled and said, “You did it, Sandi! We’re back on course!”

“We might just make it to Mars on time after all!” Tom cheered, high-fiving Sandi.

As the days passed, Sandi took great joy in learning about Mars and the preparations they would need for their exploration. The crew even practiced planting seeds in Martian soil simulations, ensuring they would grow even in the red planet's rugged conditions.

Finally, the day arrived. They could see Mars growing larger out of the rocket's windows as they approached the planet. Sandi's heart raced with excitement.

"I can't believe we're really going to land!"

When the Starlight Voyager touched down on the Martian surface, the crew cheered. Sandi stepped out and found herself on the stunning red landscape, the sun casting an orange glow across the rocky terrain.

As the team collected soil samples and went exploring, they came across rocky formations and valleys. Sandi's mind buzzed with ideas and discoveries, and the crew turned to her whenever they encountered challenges.

“What do we do next, Sandi?” Ellie asked, her eyes wide with admiration.

“Let’s set up a base camp right here,” Sandi suggested confidently. “We can do experiments and study the soil samples to see if they could support plants.”

As she worked alongside the other astronauts, sharing her insights and guiding them through various tasks, Sandi realized how invaluable this experience was.

She had finally found her place among these brilliant minds, and for the first time, she felt fully accepted for who she was.

After weeks of exploration, the team gathered all their data and shared the findings with scientists back on Earth. The mission had been a resounding success!

Sandi felt a wave of pride wash over her as she absorbed the discoveries they had made.

When it was time to return home, the crew boarded the rocket with hearts full of excitement. As they approached Earth, Sandi and her mother chatted about everything they had explored, from Martian rocks to the secrets of the stars.

When they landed back home in Brightview, the streets were alive with celebration. Fireworks lit up the sky, and a ticker-tape parade awaited them.

The townspeople had gathered to honor the astronauts for their bravery and discoveries.

Sandi stepped out of the rocket to a thunderous applause. Bright banners waved, and cheerful faces beamed with joy.

“Welcome back, Sandi! You’re our hero!” shouted a neighbor, holding a sign that read: “Sandi the Space Explorer!”

As she waved to the crowd, Sandi spotted the kids from school who had once ignored her. They all held up signs of love and friendship, and Sandi’s heart swelled with happiness.

Standing beside her mom, Sandi realized that she had embraced her uniqueness and pursued her passion. She had gone from feeling different to being celebrated, not just for being smart, but for being kind, adventurous, and brave.

Sandi looked around at the smiling faces, feeling grateful for the journey that had brought her to this moment. It was not just the adventures in space that made her special; it was the connections she had made along the way.

And as she stared up at the beautiful night sky, Sandi knew that her journey had only just begun. There were still endless discoveries waiting for her, and with the support of her friends and family, she felt ready to explore whatever came next.

Campfire Tails

On a starry summer night in the magical Maplewood Forest, the heavens shimmered with countless stars twinkling like diamonds scattered across a velvet sky. The moon cast a gentle silver glow over the towering trees, their leaves whispering secrets as a soft breeze drifted through the forest.

Amid this enchanting scenery, six young friends gathered around a warm campfire, their hearts brimming with excitement.

Mike, Joe, Tom, Liz, Rosie, and Ellie were thrilled; their beloved summer camping tradition of storytelling was about to begin! The crackling flames danced and flickered, illuminating the faces of the children, casting cheerful shadows on the trees surrounding them.

The scent of roasting marshmallows filled the air as a chorus of night sounds—crickets chirping, owls hooting, and rustling leaves—created a symphony of nature that embraced the summer night.

As they settled closer to the fire, the friends noticed flickers of movement in the underbrush. Curious eyes peeked out from behind trees and bushes, and one by one, the forest animals emerged slowly, wondering who these six humans were that had ventured into their home.

“Look! We have guests!” Tom exclaimed, pointing toward a family of deer cautiously approaching the glow of the fire, their ears perked with curiosity.

A fluffy rabbit hopped nearby, while a raccoon with masked eyes flicked its tail, intrigued by the warm light.

“Hey, little friends! Come join us!” Liz beckoned gently, her voice as inviting as the fire itself.

But the animals remained shy, hovering at the edges of the clearing. A gentle bear cub took a few steps closer, but when Ellie clapped her hands in cheer, he darted back into the safety of the trees.

“We should entertain them instead!” Mike suggested, glancing at his friends. “Let’s tell them our best stories; maybe that’ll coax them out!”

Joe jumped in with a challenge. “How about we make this even more fun! Why not split into teams: boys against girls? Let’s see who can tell the most amazing tales tonight!”

The girls exchanged looks, ready for a friendly competition.

“You’re on, Joe!” Rosie said, grinning widely.

“Let’s show them what we’ve got!” Liz declared.

“Who wants to go first?” asked Joe, a grin spreading across his face.

“I do!” Rosie chimed in, excited to share her tale. “Gather around, forest friends!”

Rosie leaned forward, and as she began her story, the flames crackled in encouragement.

“Once upon a time in a hidden part of Maplewood Forest, there lived a brave little squirrel named Max. Max had the biggest dreams of all: to discover the Great Acorn, a legendary treasure said to give any squirrel boundless energy!”

The creatures around the campfire perked their ears, captivated by Rosie’s words.

“Max loved adventures, and one bright morning, he set off with his best friend, Tina the rabbit. Together, they bravely climbed the tallest trees, leaped from branch to branch, and scampered through the rustling leaves, determined to find the Great Acorn. Along their journey, they met wise old Mr. Owl, who shared clues about the acorn’s whereabouts, leading them to the roaring river.”

Rosie paused for dramatic effect, glancing at the animals, who seemed entranced.

“But the river was filled with dangerous whirlpools! Max and Tina needed to cross safely. With quick thinking, they fashioned a raft from fallen branches and leaves. Just as they set off, a storm came in, causing the river to surge!”

The children gasped as Rosie animatedly acted out the waves crashing against the raft.

“Max, holding on tight, called to Tina, ‘We will make it! We must believe we can!’ As they paddled furiously using their tiny paws, they reached the other side just in time. They celebrated with a joyful dance, and it was then that Max realized it wasn’t just the acorn that made their adventures great, but the friendship they shared!”

As Rosie finished her story, a warm wind blew through the clearing. To her surprise, a fluffy, bushy tail began to sprout from her backside, shimmering like the dawn light. With a delighted squeal, Rosie touched her newfound squirrel tail, adorned with a tuft of golden fur that looked like sunlight.

“Look, I have a squirrel tail!” she exclaimed, twirling around, and the forest friends cheered for her excitement.

Next, it was Mike’s turn. “Let me tell you about an adventure with a very special fox!”

As Mike began his tale, a red fox cautiously stepped forward, drawn to his voice.

“Once in the forest, there lived a clever fox named Finn, known for his brilliant tricks. One day, Finn heard from a wise old turtle that an enchanted gem hidden in a field called the Silent Glade could grant wishes to those who found it. He decided to embark on a quest to find the gem, which was protected by a wise old guardian named Elder Bear.”

Mike continued, illustrating Finn's escapades. "Finn cleverly outsmarted trolls and raced through meadows filled with flowers. But his true challenge came when he met Elder Bear, who asked Finn to answer a riddle.

'What has four legs in the morning, two legs at noon, and three legs in the evening?' Finn thought hard, remembering tales from his mother about how humans walked."

"The answer is… man!" Mike shouted. "With a hearty laugh, Elder Bear presented Finn with the gem, because he proved his cleverness! Finn wished for the happiness of all his forest friends, creating a magical bond among them that lasted forever."

As Mike concluded his story, a radiant fox tail sprouted from him, flicking and playful. The animals let out happy sounds, thrilled with each story shared.

Feeling inspired by the magic they had already created, Ellie spoke next, her eyes gleaming. “I want to tell the story of a wondrous adventure in the clouds!”

The forest friends leaned in closer as Ellie’s words painted a beautiful canvas.

“In a hidden valley, lived a brave little owl named Olivia. She wanted to fly higher than any owl ever had, close enough to talk to the stars! One magical night, she met a wise old comet named Celestia who taught her about the Rainbow Winds—breezes that carried creatures from one wonder to another.

“With the help of her friends, she crafted beautiful wings from moonbeam feathers! Together, they soared into the night sky, giggling and swirling among the stars. Olivia reached the highest tip of the comet’s tail, spreading joy to all the forest animals below. The stars twinkled in applause, and from that day on, Olivia became a guiding star for every dreamer who dared chase the skies.”

As Ellie shared her story, a brilliant feathery tail sprouted from her, bright and shimmering with hues of blue and purple.

With every tale, more and more animals crept closer to the fire, enchanted by the magic of friendship and creativity woven into each story.

“Now it’s my turn!” shouted Tom, eager to continue the adventure. “Let’s go to the Crystal Cave, where a curious little badger named Benny lived!”

Tom created elaborate scenes filled with excitement. “Benny was not an ordinary badger; he had a special gift for finding hidden treasures. One day, while exploring near the sparkling River of Lights, he stumbled upon a mysterious cave glowing with shimmering crystals. Captivated, Benny couldn’t resist going inside!”

The animals gasped, their small hearts racing in sync.

"Inside the cave, Benny found a magical world filled with brightly glowing gems, singing waterfalls, and friendly elves. But lurking in the shadows was a grumpy troll, determined to keep the cave's treasures for himself! Benny knew he had to find a way to outsmart the troll."

With cleverness, Benny engaged the troll in a riddle contest while the small elves worked together to create a beautiful melody that echoed in the cave.

"In the end, Benny's wits and the elves' music defeated the troll! Benny shared the treasures with all the woodland creatures, and the cave became a sanctuary filled with warmth and laughter!"

As Tom finished, a magnificent striped badger tail appeared behind him, adorned with glimmers of silver.

As the stories unfolded, it became clear that the girls were weaving more remarkable tales, each brimming with imagination. Liz took a deep breath and spun her story.

“In a grove filled with singing flowers, a gentle deer named Dalia lived. Dalia wasn’t just any deer. She possessed the unique ability to understand the language of flowers.”

The animals perked up at the mention of Dalia.

“One day, she noticed that the flowers were wilting. Their songs grew fainter as they cried out for her help. Understanding their concerns, Dalia set out to investigate why the earth was sad. Deep in the heart of the forest, she discovered a dark, ugly thornbush choking the life out of the soil.”

“Determined to help, Dalia enlisted the help of all her animal friends to clear the thornbush and bring sunlight back. They tugged and pulled until, with one great heave, the bush collapsed! The earth sighed in relief, and the flowers burst into bloom, brighter than ever!"

With each twist and turn of the tale, a beautiful spotted deer tail elegantly grew from Liz, shimmering with petals and soft dew.

"I have one more story to tell!" Rosie exclaimed vigorously. "This is a tale about Amelia, the clever little fox."

"The other animals always called Amelia the 'whispering fox' because she could hear the smallest sounds. One evening, she overheard a group of hunters planning to come into the forest. She raced through the woods, gathering her friends to form a plan! Louie the rabbit thumped out a beat as she gathered ideas from all the creatures."

"Together, they created a huge maze of thickets, rocks, and wind songs that would confuse the hunters. And guess what?" Rosie's eyes twinkled as she leaned in.

“When the hunters came, they got completely lost! The forest animals cheered for Amelia, and as a thank you, the Great Spirit of the Forest gifted her with a luminous golden tail, signifying her courage!”

As Rosie finished her lively tale, her beautiful fox tail sparkled like a woodland fairy’s wand! The animals cheered for the girls’ fantastic stories, moving closer to the fire, ready to show their appreciation.

In the atmosphere of friendly competition, Mike realized it was time to bring their storytelling challenge to a close. As he looked at his friends, he couldn’t help but feel that everyone had told remarkable stories that showcased their imagination and kindness.

“Girls, you definitely owned the night with your creativity!” Mike said sincerely. “I have to declare the girls the winners!”

The forest echoed with joy as the animals jumped and cheered for the girls' team. Delighted by their victory, they excitedly approached the girls, nudging closer to the warmth of the fire while wagging their tails playfully.

"Thank you, forest friends!" Liz smiled, petting a shy deer that nuzzled her hand. "We couldn't have asked for better company!"

As the animal friends pressed closer, the girls beamed, their hearts swelling with happiness.

The stars twinkled brightly above as the night wore on, and the gentle sounds of the forest washed over them like a melody. Before long, one by one, the forest animals began to drift back into the safety of the woods, satisfied and full of content.

"Let's send them off!" Ellie suggested and waved goodbye to their furry friends.

As the last of the animals slipped back into the shadows, the girls decided to mark their victory. They raised their marshmallow sticks high, the sweet, gooey treats glistening in the firelight. “Girl Power!” they exclaimed in unison, laughter echoing into the night sky.

The End

Another fun book by Michael Gunning with an empowering message for young girls is the outer space adventure **Orfin Bob and the Thomas Twins**, available on Amazon. The following is an excerpt.

Orfin Bob and the Thomas Twins; The Adventure Begins

By Michael Gunning

Chapter 1
Pottsville

Pottsville is a nice little town. It has a main street, lined with old oak trees on both sides. It has a little park in the center of town, across the street from the old Bell Tower, which now serves as City Hall.

That's where Mayor Harper works, and as long as Jasmin & Jesse Thomas could remember, he was always the Mayor of Pottsville. Next door to City Hall was

Meyers General Store, and as always, there was Mr. Meyers, sweeping the sidewalk in front of his store. Everyone in town had to agree, Mr. Meyers had the cleanest sidewalk in town.

Jacob's Candy Store was just past that, and that's where Jasmin and her twin brother Jesse were heading.

Every Friday Mr. Thomas, or Dad, as Jasmin & Jesse called him, would drive the whole family to town. If they had a good week in school (which, truth be told, wasn't often), he would give them a quarter each to spend in the candy store.

While Jasmin & Jesse went to get candy, Mom would visit old Mrs. Winaragger, who owned the Beauty Shop, and Dad would go see his friend, Stan Danley, who owned the hardware store and always had the latest and best new power tools for sale.

“Now don’t get too much taken off, dear,” Dad called to Mom, as she was entering the Beauty Shop.

“I won’t honey, and remember, no more power tools,” she called back.

Dad’s shoulders slumped as he heard her words. He stood there for a moment, trying to think of a good reason to tell her he needed another super powered thingamajig to hang in his workshop, but the words wouldn’t come.

“Uh, Dad?” Jesse said, interrupting his thoughts.

Dad looked down to see Jasmin & Jesse standing there, each with their hand held out for their reward of a quarter. Dad reached into his pocket and pulled out two new shiny quarters, one for each of them.

Then Dad patted them both on the head, told them to come right back to the hardware store after getting their candy, turned and entered the store. Jasmin & Jesse ran down the sidewalk towards Jacob's Candy Store.

"I hope Mrs. Jacobs is working today," said Jesse as they approached the store.

"Me too," replied his sister, "she never counts the candy right!"

They both giggled as they entered the store. As they made it to the counter, giant smiles crossed their faces.

"Hi Mrs. Jacobs!" they both exclaimed.

“Why, there you two are!” she exclaimed. “I haven’t seen you two in two weeks. Have you been sick?”

Jesse looked at the floor and shuffled his feet.

“No, Ma’am,” he answered.

“No, huh? Hmm, then you I guess you were on a vacation?” asked Mrs. Jacobs.

Jasmin looked ashamed and shuffled her feet too.
“No Ma’am.”
“Well, you weren’t sick, and you weren’t away to some far off exciting place. That only leaves one thing, doesn’t it?”

“Yes Ma’am,” they answered together.

“So tell me, just what kind of mischief has found you two?”

“It was Jesse’s fault,” said Jasmin, pointing an accusing finger at her brother.

“No it wasn’t, well maybe last week it was, but the week before that it was all your fault,” answered Jesse, his finger pointed to match his sister’s.

“Now, now, we don’t tell tales here, children. Jesse, you go first, what kind of trouble have you been in?”

“Well,” he started. “It really wasn’t my fault. I caught a frog near Potts Lake and I brought it into school to show my friends.” “Well that certainly sounds innocent enough,” said Mrs. Jacobs.

“Yeah, until he put it in Mrs. Appleton’s desk drawer,” answered Jasmin. “When she opened her drawer to get a piece of chalk, it jumped right out, and boy, did she scream!”

Jesse couldn’t hold back his laughter. “Poor ole’ Mrs. Appleton jumped right up on top of her desk. She wouldn’t come down until the janitor came by and caught the little guy, and released him out behind the school,” said Jesse through tears of laughter.

“Why, that’s not very nice, not very nice at all,” said Mrs. Jacobs, trying her best to sound stern, and not doing a very good job of it. “You two should be ashamed…”

“I didn’t have anything to do with it, Mrs. Jacobs,” said Jasmin. “It was all Jesse that time.”

"I see, so you didn't get into any trouble yourself?" asked Mrs. Jacobs.

"Well, maybe a little bit," said Jasmin. "But nothing that had anything to do with live animals!"

"She threw bubble gum in Mrs. Applebee's hair!" exclaimed Jesse.

"Not on purpose!" Jasmin shot back. "It was an accident."

"How is throwing bubble gum an accident?" asked Mrs. Jacobs.

"Well, you see, I made a paper airplane, but it needed some weight in the front to fly right. So I chewed up some gum and stuck it to the front of the plane," explained Jasmin.

“It flew great too, a double loopity loop, and a perfect inverted dive, right into Mrs. Applebee’s hair!” laughed Jesse.

Mrs. Jacobs tried her hardest not to laugh. “Your teachers deserve a big raise, that’s all I can say. Now, how about I get you two rascals some candy. The usual?”

“Ah, yes ma’am, that would be great. We each have a quarter, is that still enough?”

“Well,” replied Mrs. Jacobs, “I think so. Let me see, these goopy gummies are a nickel each, so I can give you five of these, and these Choco-Marshmallow Bears are 10 cents each, so I can give you 5 of these too, and let me see, some of these, and some of these, and there, that outta do it.”

Mrs. Jacobs held up two small bags full of candy. “Now let me add this up. Hmm, some of these, plus two of these, and five of these, equals…” she scratched her head while thinking hard. “Why, it comes to fifty cents on the dot!” exclaimed Mrs. Jacobs. “Am I good or what?”

Both children giggled.

“You sure are Mrs. Jacobs, you sure are,” Jasmin said.

The children left the store and ran down the sidewalk towards the hardware store. They sat on the curb just outside the front door and started to eat the candy, as always, Gummies first.

Chapter 2
Killing Boredom

Living in Pottsville was nice, and Jasmin & Jesse were almost completely content. Almost because, truth be told, with the exception of playing on the swings in the playground, and catching frogs by Potts Lake, and going to Jacob's Store for candy, and playing hide and seek with their friends, and, well, just about every other kind of fun you can think of, Jasmin and Jesse were bored.

"We need to do something fun," Jesse said, as he skipped a rock across the surface of Potts Lake. "Here we are on a

Saturday afternoon with nothing to do, no place to go, no one to see…"

"Like what Jesse?" asked Jasmin, "There isn't a lot to do around here…at least not a lot that we can't get into trouble for." Jesse sat on a tree stump, scratching his forehead with his index finger. "Let me think about this for a minute, I'll come up with something."

Jasmin & Jesse sat in silent thought for a few minutes. Suddenly, Jasmin sat up and said, "I've got it. We could climb Mrs. Higgenbottem's tree and drop water balloons on passing cars."

"Jasmin, we need to stay out of trouble," said Jesse, killing the idea.

"Well, how about we play dress up?" suggested Jasmin.

“No way, last time you covered me with make-up, made me put on that dress and put that silly doll in my hands, just as David and the guys came over to ask me to play football. Do you know how long it took for them to ask me to play football with them again? They kept calling me Powder Puff Boy. Never again. Never ever again.”

Jesse sat there shaking his head at the memory. Suddenly, his eyes lit up.

“I know, let’s go ask Mom and Dad if we can set up the tent in the backyard and go camping tonight!” exclaimed Jesse.

“Camping in the backyard? Total dullsville, Jesse.”

“I know, but not if we sneak out to the bogs over by Potts Field. There’s a full moon tonight, and if we get real lucky, maybe we’ll hear the Bog Monsters slushing through the mud,” Jesse said with a sly smile on his face.

“C’mon, there is no such thing as a Bog Monster…I think,” replied Jasmin, a little nervously.

“Uh huh, I heard Dad talking ’bout it with Mr. Danley at the hardware store. They were talking about how Farmer Waller lost a couple of cows last summer, and they think it was the Bog Monsters that got ’em.”

“No way, really?” asked Jasmin, now very nervously. “I don’t know Jesse, didn’t you just say we need to stay outta trouble?”

“We won’t get caught, Mom and Dad sleep like logs. Besides, we can hear Dad snoring from halfway across town. No way will we get caught.”

Dad had the tent set up in no time, and Mom brought out the sleeping bags, still warm from the dryer after a washing to freshen them up. She carefully unrolled them on the floor of the tent, then fluffed the pillows with the fresh pillowcases and laid them gently on top of the sleeping bags.

“Now, you’re sure you don’t want us to stay out here with you?” asked Dad. “You won’t be scared?”

“Thanks Dad, but we know you’re right inside. Besides, we got Spaulding here to protect us.”

At the sound of his name, Spaulding, the family's big old half Doberman, half Great Dane mix cocked his head from side to side, then walked over to Jesse and nudged his hand with his nose. Jesse rubbed him on the head.

"You'll protect us, won't you boy?" asked Jesse, as he knelt down in front of the dog.

Spaulding licked his face once, and nuzzled him in the chest, knocking Jesse backwards. Then he pounced on him, causing Jesse to laugh.

As big as he was, Spaulding knew that he had to be careful when playing with his humans. He was so big, Jasmin and Jesse used to both ride on his back like a horse when they were younger. Now he could only carry them one at a time, which he still delighted in doing when mom would allow it.

“He’s getting too old for that,” Mom would warn them, but the truth was he was still as strong as ever.

“OK you two, no more playing. Time to get yourselves some sleep,” Mom said.

Jesse stood up, kissed Mom, and then gave his dad a big hug. Jasmin followed, kissing both of them. Then she climbed into her sleeping bag next to Jesse, with Spaulding lying down between them.

“You won’t be too cold, will you dear?” asked Mom.

“I’ll be fine Mommy, now stop worrying. I’m a big girl now. I mean, gosh, we are almost 12, you know,” Jasmin said.

“OK, but if you get too cold, or scared, or….”

Dad interrupted her. “Let’s go dear, stop being a mother hen. Let the children have their night out under the sky. Nothing is going to mess with them out here, not with Spaulding guarding them, right boy?”

Dad knelt and gave Spaulding one last rub behind the ears.

“Arroof,’ Spaulding replied, as if to say “No worries, Pop! These two are as safe as could be with me!”

Mom and Dad walked into the house, and before long, Jasmin & Jesse could hear the rhythm of Dad’s snores, telling them he was sound asleep.

Chapter 3
Sneaking Off

With Mom and Dad sound asleep, Jasmin & Jesse climbed out of the tent and quietly tiptoed over to the back fence. They opened the back gate quietly, and with Spaulding trotting along, they took off for Potts Field.

With the moon full and bright, it was easy to find the old trail that went through the woods to Potts Field, right across from where the Bog started. Although the trail was dry, the ground around it was soft from the rain two days before.

"Lets cut through here, it's a short cut," suggested Jesse.

"It might be muddy out there, Jesse. I think we should stay on the trail," Jasmin cautiously warned him.

Jesse was already leaving the trail, with Spaulding on his heels.

"C'mon, I know the way."

Jasmin shook her head. "Oh Jesse. Why won't you ever listen to me?"

Jasmin followed Jesse off the trail, walking quickly to catch up.

"Are you sure you know where we're going?" asked Jasmin.

“Of course I do. Trust me.” Jesse said reassuringly.

“Trust you? Like the time you told me to trust you when you put that food on my plate and told me it was beef hash, and you really gave me dog food? Yuck, I can still taste it.”

“You ate the whole thing, didn’t you?” laughed Jesse.

“Just don’t go too fast, OK, Jesse? I don’t like being in these woods in the dark.”

Jasmin & Jesse continued to walk through the woods, the sound of crickets ringing in their ears. The occasional hoot of an owl would be answered by a short low bark by Spaulding, as if to say, “Stay away. These are my humans!”

After a while, Jasmin started to get worried. “Jesse, I think you got us lost.”

“Jasmin, I think you worry too much. The field is right past those two trees up there. I could walk these woods blindfolded!” Jesse replied, trying to sound brave.

Jasmin doubted him, but kept going. After all, it was too far to go back, and even though she didn’t want Jesse to know it, she was getting afraid. They came to the trees Jesse spoke of, and walked past them, right into…more woods.

“Jesse, you did get us lost!” Jasmin said, fighting back tears. “I want to go home, Jesse, I want to go home now!”

Jesse grabbed his sister’s hand. “Don’t worry Jasmin, we’ll find our way out of here. I must have made a wrong turn somewhere. Just hold my hand, and everything will be fine. Now which way did we come from?"

After walking for a few minutes, Jesse kicked a small stone with his foot.

"Look, a perfect skipping stone!"

Jesse bent over to pick up the rock. It was smooth and flat, perfect for a toss across Potts Lake.

"Would you please leave the stones alone and get us out of here, Jesse," pleaded Jasmin.

"OK, OK," replied Jesse.

He flipped the rock in his hand a few times, and then cocked his arm back. "See that airplane way up there? Bet you I can hit it!"

Jesse hurled the stone upwards, towards the lights of an airplane flying way overhead. Suddenly, out of nowhere, there was a loud bang, followed by a bright ball of light which flew just over the treetops above their heads, whistling loudly, and Jasmin & Jesse watched as it crashed into the woods in front of them.

"Watch out!" Jesse screamed, as he pushed his sister to the ground and threw himself on top of her.

Debris fell from the sky all around them, covering them with muddy clumps of bog dirt. Jesse covered Jasmin's face to protect her from the falling mud. After a few moments, when things settled down,

Jesse stood up and helped his sister to her feet.

Spaulding crawled between Jesse's legs, and all three looked in the direction of the strange crash.

"Now you've really done it Jesse. You knocked an airplane out of the sky. Mom and Dad are going to ground us for a week!" Jasmin said.

"I couldn't have. I didn't throw it that hard. I never thought I would really hit it," answered Jesse. "We need to go look, see if anyone was hurt."

"No Jesse, I don't want to go, I'm really scared. Really, really scared." Jasmin looked as if she was going to start crying.

“Don’t cry Jasmin, nothing is going to happen. I’m just going to look, that’s all. Besides, if someone did get hurt, we’d feel awful bad for not helping them.”

Jesse took a few steps towards the crash area, and Jasmin grabbed his arm, holding his hand tightly.

“I’m not staying here alone,” said Jasmin. “Boy, I’m definitely telling Mom on you for this one.”

Chapter 4
Trees Don't Talk, Do They?

Jasmin & Jesse walked cautiously towards the crash site, not sure what to expect. Jasmin could feel Jesse's hand shaking in hers. They climbed carefully over some fallen trees and came to a large hole in the ground.

The hole was full of smoke, with some drifting out over the sides.

"Is anyone in there?' Jesse called nervously.

"Is anyone in there?" a voice called back.

Jesse and Jasmin jumped back.

“Oh Jesse, I want to get out of here, please, please, take me home,” Jasmin begged.

“Please, please, take me home,” the same voice said.

“Jasmin, I think it’s just an echo. Listen. Hello, helloooo,” Jesse called.

“Hello, helloooo,” the voice called back.

Jesse turned to Jasmin. “See, just an echo. Nothing to worry about.”

“Hello, helloooo.” the voice called again.

Jasmin & Jesse turned to each other, their eyes as big as saucers.

“BOG MONSTERS!!” they shouted.

Spaulding yelped, and all three of them turned and ran, Jasmin & Jesse screaming at the top of their lungs.

Behind them they could hear the voice.

“Hello, helloooo, BOG MONSTERS!! AAAHHHHH. Hello Helloooo, Please, Please take me home. BOG MONSTERS!! Hello, Helloooo.”

The voice was getting louder, and Jesse could hear the Bog Monster coming after them, taunting them.

“Hello, helloooo, BOG MONSTERS!!, AAAHHHHH. Hello Helloooo, Please, Please take me home. BOG MONSTERS!! Hello, Helloooo.”

“Run, Jasmin, Run!” pleaded Jesse. “It’s going to eat us!”

Up ahead, Spaulding stopped and turned.

He growled and started barking, and Jasmin & Jesse ran right by him. They ran past a giant old oak tree, and Jesse grabbed Jasmin's hand and pulled her behind it, hiding them both.

They scrunched down as low as they could, both out of breath as much from fear as from the running. They could hear Spaulding barking, and Jasmin realized the voice had stopped.

After a few seconds, Spaulding stopped barking, and Jesse peaked around the side of the tree.

"Jesse, no! It'll see you!"

“Shhh, Jasmin. I have to see if Spaulding’s OK.”

Jesse stuck his head out a little further, and there was Spaulding, tail wagging, staring at the strangest looking tree Jesse had ever seen. The Bog Monster was nowhere to be found. Jesse started to stand up.

“What are you doing?” Jasmin asked.

“It’s gone, Spaulding scared it away.” Jesse said as he walked out from behind the tree.

“Good boy, Spaulding, Good boy.” Jesse walked slowly over to Spaulding, looking around to see if the Bog Monster was also hiding behind a tree. He got to Spaulding and knelt beside him. Jasmin came up from behind and also knelt down. She gave the dog a big hug.

“Oh, Spaulding, you’re such a good boy. You saved us,” said Jasmin, as she gave him another hug. “Now, if you can just find the way home.”

Jasmin & Jesse got up. “Which way? asked Jasmin.

“I don’t know. I guess we should just keep going this way,” said Jesse, as he pointed towards the direction they were running.

They started to walk, but Spaulding continued to stand there, glaring at the strange looking tree, a low, deep growl rumbling from his chest.

“What is it boy?” asked Jasmin. “Are you OK?” then to Jesse, “Is he OK?”

“I think so, he doesn’t look hurt,” replied Jesse. “What’s so special about that weird looking tree?”

Spaulding turned to face Jesse, then turned back to the tree. “Grrr, Ruff” barked Spaulding.

The tree jumped back a foot when Spaulding barked.

“Did you just see what I think I just saw?” asked Jesse.

“If you mean that tree just took a step backward, then no, there’s just no way I saw that,” answered Jasmin.

“Grrr, ruff, ruff” Spaulding barked again. The tree moved again.

“Whoa, I know I just saw it that time. OK. Who’s doing that?” Jesse asked, as he bent over to pick up a small tree branch. “I have a stick, and I’m not afraid to use it!”

“I’m not afraid to use it.” said the voice again.

“Who said that?” Jesse demanded. He looked around, holding the stick ready to swing at anything.

“Jesse, I uh…” started Jasmin.

“What, Jasmin, did you say it?”

“I uh, think the tree said it,” Jasmin replied.

“The tree said it, the tree said it,” said the tree.

Jasmin and Jesse looked at each other in amazement.

“No Way!!” yelled Jesse. “A talking tree!!” Jesse turned towards Jasmin. “We’ll be rich!!”

“We’ll be rich, we’ll be rich!” said the tree.

Purchase this book on Amazon to continue to follow Jesse and his sister Jasmin as they meet and befriend Orfin Bob, a shape changing alien from the Planet Orf, and go on some of the wildest adventures across the universe, and still make it home in time for dinner!